SWORDS
BOOK FOUR OF THE

Robert Ryan

Copyright © 2022 Robert J. Ryan
All Rights Reserved. The right of Robert J. Ryan to be identified as the author of this work has been asserted. All of the characters in this book are fictitious and any resemblance to actual persons, living or dead, is coincidental.

Cover design by www.damonza.com

ISBN: 9798353875178
(print edition)

Trotting Fox Press

Contents

1. Ten Thousand in Gold	3
2. A Hollow Victory	11
3. A Path Laid Out	18
4. A Badge of Honor	27
5. Ambush	37
6. I Must Do It	48
7. Give Me Your Word	56
8. The Cover of Night	60
9. Divide the Enemy's Power	65
10. Secrets	71
11. We Have Been Found	78
12. The Eyes of the Enemy	83
13. The Vision of the Blades	92
14. The Warning of the Skulls	100
15. Committed to Battle	106
16. A Terror of the Old World	114
17. A Frenzy of Madness	120
18. Hail, Brother!	128
19. The Blessing of the Queen	136
20. The Witch-healer	143
21. Nagrak City	153
22. The Fear of Magic	163
23. Old Men of the Dim Past	168
24. Are You Worthy?	176
25. To the Death	183
Appendix: Encyclopedic Glossary	194

1. Ten Thousand in Gold

Drogul, Seventh Elder of the Conclave of Shamans, Speaker of the Rites, Keeper of the History, knew fear.

Curiosity was its shadow, for this was a circumstance that had not arisen before. Yet it was curiosity of the kind that was dangerous. He tried to seek the passionless embrace of Heart of the Hurricane, the refuge of the warrior and shaman alike, to shield him from emotions that would pull his mind one way and then the other. Doing so, he could make whatever decisions were to come based on reason alone. But he failed.

The hearth in his study burned steadily, but neither fire nor warmth gave comfort. The envelope in his hands was light, yet it seemed to him to drag toward the floor with the weight of a mountain. He should cast it into the flames unread, for nothing good would come of opening it. Yet he could not do that. It must be read.

Still, he hesitated. He gazed into the fire, and watched a log turn momentarily blue-red as a wave of flame ran along its length. The hearth was large enough to fit several such logs, being both deep and wide. It was a thing of beauty, crafted in ages past as a place where several people might easily sit before it in comfort. And if the fire did not hold their gazes, the marble mantelpiece and jambs to each side would. The marble was carved with scenes from Cheng history dating back to the Shadowed Wars, and they were gilded with skill and delicacy that was beyond Cheng craftsmen of this age to match.

Scenes of battle, conquered enemies, harvests of the fields and the gods were a frequent motif, yet at the top and center, beautiful and terrible, were the very king and queen of the pantheon, and these were not just of gold but decorated also with precious gems and colored lead. It seemed to Drogul that the gods themselves were there, studying him in turn with their bright eyes catching the smoldering lights of the fire.

The beauty of the hearth was enough to make the heart flutter, yet he barely saw it, and still he felt no warmth. The dread of the letter in his hand drained away all else.

He must open it. He took the gold letter opener from the silver tray the servant had brought him the envelope on, and studied the outside once more to ensure he had not made a mistake the first time he looked.

It was addressed to him. By name. Yet none outside the order of shamans *knew* his name. Not his true one, at least. Nor would a shaman write to him. Magic allowed quicker communication, and without any risk that others might see what was written and learn what they should not.

Not only did the envelope bear his name, but it also displayed his rank as Seventh Elder, which was a title not used outside the circle of shamans and forbidden knowledge for the general populace. Even had a shaman written to him, that title would never be revealed.

It was not a shaman who wrote to him though. He knew that, and that was what made his blood run cold. Making himself do so again, he turned over the envelope to study its back.

It was sealed with blue wax such as a chieftain might use, but they seldom, if ever as far as he knew, impressed into that wax any markings that signified their office or family house. Yet right there before him he saw such a thing.

His heart beat slowly. The insignia was one that he knew, and he knew whence it came: the pommel stone of the Sword of Dawn. It was of two crossed swords, and it was the mark of the old emperor that had not been seen in a thousand years.

Shar Fei had written to him, and he could not guess why. He was as bitter an enemy to her as any other shaman. Still less could he understand how she had known where he lived, his name or his rank. That she knew these things was cause for fear. What else did she know? How was it possible that she knew anything about him at all?

His mind drifted back to ages past. He had known the Emperor Chen Fei. Certainly he was young at the time, but he had been alive. He had risen high since then, and attained a position on the Conclave. He was more powerful by far, yet to know that one of Chen Fei's blood still walked the earth was knowledge that weighed on him with dread. He had known Olekhai. He had been a junior member of the delegation that bribed the prime minister and influenced him to assassinate the emperor. Could Shar possibly know *that*? If she did, and she knew where he lived, would she seek his death?

He would not underestimate her. Many had, but she had won a following in the east and victories in battle. She had killed shamans and chieftains alike. If she came for him, she would be dangerous.

Taking a firm grip on the letter opener he ran it through the paper, then pulled out the correspondence. It was on fine paper, and written in a neat script such as a scribe for a chieftain might use. Then he looked away and tried to prepare himself. He could not guess what her message would be, yet whatever it was it would not be for the faint of heart.

Again he wondered how she had known his address, but whoever had delivered it could not be questioned. The envelope had been passed under the front door of the mansion during the night and not found until the servants roused this morning.

He forced himself to read it at last.

Hail, Drogul, Elder of the Conclave and murderer of men, women and children. I know your history, your crimes, and the deeds you have done to rise to your position. I know all, and justice pursues you, even if a thousand years too slowly.

Already, the east is mine. North, south and west will follow. The four corners of the land will hem you in like prison bars, and within the borders of the Cheng Empire I shall seek you out and have you hanged. No cave, nor cottage nor mansion will hide you. Only the grave will cover you over.

Mayhap you know I have already visited this justice upon some of your brethren. More will follow. One day you will dance the same jig as they.

Truly, the shamans are accursed, and I shall cleanse the land of your evil. You think victory belongs to you, but a thousand years is nothing to the call of vengeance and the loyalty of blood.

Go hence and warn your comrades. I am coming. An army marches with me, and destiny is my shadow. You may flee, or fight, but all your roads lead to ruin. It was thus the moment you tried, and failed, to expunge an entire family from the land. Not only are you evil - you are incompetent also.

I have spoken. Deeds will follow. When we meet, I shall have rope ready. I know all that you do, and what the Conclave plans. No secret is hidden from me. If you doubt this, look up at the gold hearth you sit before. Is it not before it that you wait of a morning while your servants ready the house?

Yours in eternal vengeance,
Shar Fei.

Drogul let the paper slip to the floor from his numb fingers, and glanced at the hearth. Then he looked sharply away and closed his eyes. He took long, slow breaths to calm his heart, which fluttered wildly in his chest.

The audacity of the girl stunned him. How *dare* she say those things, and yet if he had ever had doubts that she was of the old emperor's blood they were vanished now. That had been the man's tone too. It was supreme arrogance, yet at the same time, it was not. From their point of view, it was always simply stating facts.

He knew what Shar had tried to do with the letter. It served no purpose, save one only. To frighten the shamans, for she knew he must report this to the Conclave, and from there it would filter down to the rest of the order. By frightening them, she hoped to precipitate errors of judgement. Panic even. That would only be to her benefit, for if she was nothing else, he could tell by the letter that she herself was a person of cool judgement and reason. Fear would not work against her, but it was a tool she could use herself. And already he could picture the outrage among the members of the Conclave. They would show no fear themselves, even if they felt it. He knew he did.

The lower ranks would feel it more. She had struck a blow here greater than any victory in battle she had already won. The shamans held the land in an iron grip, yet if they faltered, if they overstepped their mark in giving orders, if they failed to be bold enough, then the people would rise to support her and topple the shamans. It was a narrow path his kind must walk to keep the status quo of the last thousand years, and Shar was throwing everything at them to send them astray. Battle. Fear. Hope to the masses. What else would she do?

No matter that she was the bitterest of enemies, he could almost admire her. She was clever. The way she had echoed the words of her dying forefather and invoked a feel that his prophecy was coming to life was shrewd. She could have overtly claimed as much, but better by far to let the shamans think that of their own accord. It was a subtle tactic. Fear from within was more disabling than fear imposed from without. The latter was instinctively fought because it was seen as manipulation. The first was accepted because it was the person's *own* thoughts.

Now that the shock of the first reading had worn off, he began to grow angry. The shamans had never been insulted like this before. Not for a thousand years, anyway. Worse, there was evidently a spy in his household. He would interrogate them all, but that would likely be a fruitless effort. There were a dozen of them, and they would all protest their innocence. They had been with him for years, and whoever it was must be skilled at deception to evade suspicion for so long.

Who could such a spy work for though? Surely not Shar. It must be Shulu Gan. She was ever a thorn in the side of the shamans, and time after time had escaped their traps. Yet the rumor was that age was at last catching up to her, and her powers were weakening.

Drogul stood, and, having regained his composure, tugged three times at the bell pull nearby. Then he sat again, being careful to pick up the letter from the floor and ensure his face was a mask of calmness.

Presently, a servant entered. It was Anakabael, whom he had always favored. He had known her for forty years, and trusted her with secrets for thirty of them. Yet his eyes narrowed now in suspicion at her plain face. She was not of Cheng origin, having been captured as a slave in her youth from lands to the south. Was it possible that she still harbored resentment at that? Could one such as she have been turned against him?

"Yes, master?" she asked, head bowed.

He studied her a moment in silence, then cast aside his doubts. He would not let Shar become a shadow in his mind, making him second guess everything and everyone.

"Have a letter drawn up. It will be to all the chieftains. After the normal formalities, let it read simply thus. Ten thousand in gold coins to anyone who kills the woman that styles herself as Shar Fei. Any shaman, anywhere, will reward you with the prize upon proof."

The woman nodded briskly. "I'll have the copies brought to you before lunch for signing." Then she bowed again and left.

Drogul gazed once more into the fire and thought. She had not seemed nervous or showed any surprise at the mention of Shar or the reward. But a spy would not have done so. At least not one who had deceived him for decades.

He wished there were a way to send word directly to the traitor chiefs who had joined the rebel army. But it did not really matter. It might take a little longer, but word of a reward that large would reach them and spread like a fire through a drought-stricken forest. If the news entered the camp with a messenger at dawn, it would be on every soldier's lips by nightfall.

For the first time that morning, he felt relaxed and smiled. The gold was nothing to the shamans. Three Moon Mountain held the treasures of the ages. Yet to every soldier in her army, to every person in the land, it was a fortune undreamed of. When Shar heard of it, she would trust no one, not even her closest friends. If she wanted to try to instill fear in the shamans, he could not stop her. He could do the same to her though, ten thousand times over.

2. A Hollow Victory

Her army rested for two days after the battle in which they had gained victory. Shar chafed at the delay, yet it was necessary.

The soldiers needed time to recuperate, and after what they had gone through she would give it to them. On the last afternoon Asana came to her in her tent, where he found her alone. Even Huigar and Radatan were absent, which was rare. She had sent them on an errand, and though they did not want to leave her side they had followed her orders.

"Enter," she called when the little bell was rung at the tent opening.

Asana walked in, taking his time and letting his eyes adjust to the lower light.

"No guards?" he asked.

She grinned at him and then patted the hilts of her swords.

"I'm risking it for an hour or so. I sent them away to check on something with the chiefs for me."

The swordmaster tilted his head slightly to one side as though in thought.

"You sent them somewhere that you knew they would be offered food, drink and cheer as the army still celebrates. That is the real reason, is it not?"

She shrugged. "They wouldn't have gone otherwise. And they deserve a rest and some merriment as much as everyone else."

"No doubt," he said, sitting in the chair she offered him. "But not you?"

"I'm busy. I've much to think on."

He looked at her shrewdly. "You're thinking about how the enemy uses sorcery against us, but we have no means to properly defend against it."

She sat back. He had pinpointed exactly what had been concerning her. It was no surprise. He knew her well, but it was also because that was the greatest weakness of her army and he, being the skilled strategist he was, would have been thinking about the same problem.

"All else has a chance of falling into place," she answered. "I can work with having a smaller army than my enemy. Momentum is on my side there, and I don't need to force a battle yet. Morale is high and supplies are good. The tribes that have come together to join me are working better and better together. Everything is in place to push forward when I choose. But we need more than just my swords and Kubodin's axe to defend against sorcery. Courage and steel aren't enough."

Asana did not change expression. He always looked relaxed and placid, yet there was something in his eyes that spoke of worry.

"Have you thought of a way yet to get us what we need? What of Shulu?"

It was a good question. She did not know what Shulu was doing, but whatever it was it would be something to help as best as possible. If she were not here, she had reasons.

"I don't know what Shulu is doing. When the time is right, we'll see her."

"And until then?"

"I do have an idea. I'm working through it. It might be the answer, but it might just create even bigger problems. I'm still turning it over in my mind."

Asana did not press her on what that plan might be, and she was glad. She was not ready to reveal it yet, for it was desperate and she might not proceed with it at all.

The next day the army moved westward. They sang as they marched for the joy of victory still infused them. They did not know exactly where they went though, and the chiefs, if the army was not, were concerned with this. They wanted a destination so they could assess their chances of further victories.

Shar was in no rush to choose though. For the moment, westward was the only way. The sea to the north and the mountains to the south made it so, but soon both would extend away from her as they passed through this relatively narrow neck of land and the heart of the Cheng Empire would open up to her.

This would also bring her close to Tsarin Fen. She ached to see her home. There were members of the Fen Wolf tribe near her now, not least Argash whom she had made chief, and that gave her comfort. Yet there was nothing like the lands that she had trodden in her youth, the smell of the swamp and the humid air. That was home as no other place ever could be. She longed to be there again.

At the same time, she had brought turmoil to the land. Chaos now swept through the tribes, and she was not sure what reception she would get. The warriors around her now were one thing. They liked her and would fight for her. That was what warriors wanted, at least the younger ones. Argash was older and wiser, but what of the families in Tsarin Fen? What of the mothers and fathers of warriors who might be killed? They would not like her, even if they wished to be free of the shamans.

It had been her dream to return to Tsarin Fen in triumph, but she had blood on her hands now. No one would look at her the same way, and even if they were friendly to her face would that be merely out of fear?

The choice of where to take the army must be made soon though. And certainly they must stop near Tsarin Fen even if she did not enter herself. Argash had to. He must show himself to the people as their new chief, win their trust and loyalty, and perhaps, convince them that Shar, though she had disrupted their lives immensely, would bring them good in the end. He might be able to do that better than she could.

There was also the matter of supplies. The army had grown, and it needed food and equipment. The first step toward bringing the Fen Wolf Tribe into her fold was *buying* such things from them. They would fear it was going to been taken by force, but a tally had been made of the loot gained from conquered chieftains and shamans, and the army had good funds. For the moment, at least.

They marched, the sun arcing through the sky, and at hourly intervals as was the custom among armies, they rested. It was better to do so briefly, but frequently, than to push ahead for too long and then to require a lengthy rest.

It was midafternoon when the grassland began to change and become less flat. It fell at a downward slope, if barely perceptibly, and that told Shar that Tsarin Fen was close.

The army rested again, and Shar sat beneath a stunted oak tree. Lightning had blasted it. Rot had eaten away at it. Its branches were covered in lichen, yet it still lived and flung out some sparse-leafed branches to catch the light. It was much like the Cheng Empire. It may have been destroyed by the shamans, yet if you scratched beneath the surface there was still life there. She had proof of that in how well her army of tribes had come together. The shamans had encouraged conflict and mistrust for a thousand years, but she had brought them together with a common purpose, and they had discovered the strength of friendship and unity.

Argash was talking to a man nearby, and when he was done she signaled for him to join her. He sat down as she had done, their backs to the tree. The trunk was not large enough that they could face the same direction.

"Do you miss the old days of simple patrols around the borders of the fen?"

She was glad then that he could not see her face. "With all my heart."

He broached the subject she had been thinking on for a while.

"We're close now. You'll see it again shortly."

It was only in that very moment that she made her decision.

"I think not. Better to keep the memories I have than change them to something less appealing. I fear to return and be … looked at differently."

Argash twisted his head around to look at her. "I don't think the people will feel less love for you. You were one of their daughters, and you have brought them glory. I think they'll love you all the more."

She was not so sure about that. She had always intended to make them proud, and to raise them from the poverty in which they lived. She had done neither yet though, and it did not feel right to her to go home until she had achieved that.

"I'll return one day, maybe. If I can. For now though, you must certainly go. Not with the army, but with an honor guard from different tribes. Let the people see that the tribes can unite. I'll send gold with you too for supplies and equipment."

He ignored all that. "You should go yourself. With the chiefs and the gold. After all, that's your achievement. Show them who you've become, and what you can do."

She sighed. "Not a day has passed since I've left that I didn't want to go back. I wanted to return and overthrow the shaman who ordered my death. Yet he came to me instead, and it's done. It seems a hollow victory to me now though."

"All victories seem hollow after their gaining. It's the way of human nature to forget the good and to dwell on the bad. Yet without those victories, where would we be?"

It was a good point, and Shar remembered why she liked this man. She had made up her mind not to go though.

The rest break was soon over, and the army marched once more. They did not sing as much as before. Their minds had now turned from the joy of surviving battle to that disquieting prospect – the future.

By afternoon of the following day they had reached the border of Tsarin Fen. Shar could see the lush growth of the swamp. She could smell it when the breeze turned and carried the hint of her homeland to her.

The army established a camp, but Shar stood still, her gaze fixed on the trees in the distance. Memories flooded through her.

She thought of her childhood, and remembered the first fish she had ever caught. The dappled light of the forest played across her mind, and she saw the faces of those she knew as she had grown up, and then those she had worked with in the Leng Fah. Some were dead now. She remembered the sweat dripping from her face as Shulu taught her to fight with sword, knife and staff. The warmth of an evening fire was in her memories too, Shulu with her legs drawn up under a blanket while she taught the history of the land.

A ghirlock bird flew away to the west, and the characteristic sound of it brought the sting of tears to her eyes. Suddenly, she realized she had been wrong to doubt that the people would welcome her home. She thought they would. The real reason she did not wish to go back was that she could not bear to see someone else now living in Shulu's cottage.

3. A Path Laid Out

Before dusk, Argash slipped away from the camp with a guard of some fifty men. It was enough to keep him safe from attack in case there were forces at home still loyal to the shamans, but it was not so much as to strike fear into the villagers.

Shar watched him go, and looked on in that direction even after the sun had set and the night had swallowed both him, and the fen, from sight. The scent of the swamp in the air became even stronger.

This would allow the soldiers another rest, and they would enjoy it. Of their enemies, Shar did not know. She had scouts out, but they reported nothing unusual. At least, as far as they had gone. She did not let them get more than a few days ahead of the army. It was safer for them that way, and that was sufficient to give her warning should an army approach.

Would there be one, though? It was a question that vexed her. Likely, the shamans had not anticipated on their first being defeated. If so, they would be scrambling now to raise another. But then what? Winter was approaching, and the season for fighting was at its tail end. They might risk it though. Cold weather, disease and death meant little to them. The shamans would not be the ones suffering any of that.

She slept poorly that night, and dreamed of the fen and running along the paths she knew so well, only to find that they had changed and she tumbled into mud and water.

The next morning dawned bright and clear, and despite the cool night it warmed quickly. Winter was coming, but there was still time for another battle.

It was another day of rest, and the army enjoyed it. Well that they should. Darker days were ahead. Shar knew that despite making a good start she was only at the beginning of this journey. More blood would be spilled yet, and without protection against sorcery her chances of victory were slim.

For now though, all was well. She gave herself no time to enjoy the rest though. Throughout the morning, she toured the camp and spoke to chiefs, soldiers and scouts alike. It was her duty to do so. They must see who she was, and come to know her. She must talk to them, and understand what was in their hearts. Especially so for those new tribes that had more recently joined their force to hers.

After lunch, she practiced her sword skills. This drew a crowd, and many watched her. Because of this, she held nothing back and performed at full speed and power. Or almost. It was not wise to let just anyone see the full extent of her skills. She held just a little back. Enough so that if there were any assassins in the camp biding their time, she might surprise them.

When she was done with the swords, she sparred Radatan and Huigar before the crowd as well, but this was done with staves, and the crack of timber was loud. The staff was not her preferred weapon, but she was still good. Huigar nearly beat her though.

At length, drenched in sweat, she called a halt and the crowd dispersed. The entertainment was over, and Shar waited for Argash's return in her tent. He should be back by nightfall, or not long after. Hopefully things had gone well. If nothing else, the gold she had given him would make sure it was so. The Fen Wolves would surely have never seen so much in hundreds of years. She just hoped they had supplies and equipment to spare over and above their own needs.

It was an hour after nightfall before Argash returned, and when he came into her tent she saw by the smile on his face that it had gone well.

"What news, Argash?"

"All good, Nakatath."

Shar was a little startled to hear him use the formal term for emperor-to-be. It seemed strange coming from one whom she had once taken orders from. Yet many of the men had started calling her this now.

Argash raised his hand and spread out his fingers and thumb.

"We found five chests of gold, gems and jewelry in the shaman's cottage. It was well hidden, buried behind his hut. At least it would have been, but we found several nazram in the act of trying to dig it up and flee. We came on them too quickly though."

Shar studied him. She saw how tired he looked, for he must barely have slept in a long while. And there was a bruise starting to show on his face as well as a scratch on his arm. There had been a fight with the nazram.

"Did we lose any soldiers?"

"None."

"And what of the other tasks?"

"They had little to spare, but we secured some equipment and a fair amount of grain. It should arrive during the course of tomorrow."

Shar offered him a goblet of wine, which he drank in a gulp.

"You did well Argash." She poured him another, which he sipped slowly this time.

"Who would have thought," he said, "that the shaman of such a poor tribe as the Fen Wolves had so much gold?"

It was certainly more than Shar thought, and her face hardened. She remembered times of famine when children had died for lack of food. And he had done nothing.

"There's more," Argash continued. "The Fen Wolves did not send all their warriors to war. It seems the previous chief held a reserve back of several hundred men. It's not a lot, but they'll be joining us tomorrow with the supplies."

Shar grinned at him. "Better and better. All your news is good!"

He did not smile in return. Rather, he now looked subdued and the smile slipped from her face.

"What is it?"

"Not all my news is good." He hesitated, then reached out to place a hand over hers on the table. "The cottage of your grandmother is burned down. I don't know who did it, or why. It happened after the Fen Wolves marched to war. There's nothing left of your old home now except some charred timbers and the stonework surrounding the hearth."

It was bad news, and terribly sad, but not as bad as it could have been.

"It seems that not everybody likes me, but a cottage is only a cottage no matter how many memories I have of living there. The main thing is that Shulu and I both escaped those who came after us. We are alive, and our battle continues. That's what counts."

Argash left soon after, and he did not see the tears glisten in her eyes while she was alone in the tent.

There were no tears the next day though when the supplies and extra men arrived. She personally looked over the equipment, and welcomed the new soldiers.

She chafed at the delay, for while her army was idle the enemy might be moving. Yet they did not know whither she intended to go, and that was to her advantage. By the mere expedient of shifting a few degrees in direction, she could add days to their journey should they intend to intercept her. But before winter set in, she intended a far greater variation in her course than that.

That evening a fire was set outside her tent, and several logs burned. It was just as the chiefs liked it for their meetings, and she called one, and they sat on one side of the fire and the breath of the gods, as they called smoke, blew over them. She did not believe, as did the hill tribes, that this gifted wisdom to their conversation, but it did no harm to respect their customs.

"We're approaching a crossroads, chiefs," she began. "Soon, things must change. But first, I would prepare the way. All over the land rumor of what this army is doing must be spreading. The people are being given hope, but farther to the west is a long way away. Rumor might be dim. And the shamans will be doing all they can to deny our victories, or downplay them. How can we better get word to spread?"

"What does it matter?" Dakashul asked.

"To us," Shar replied, "nothing definite. However, if rumor of our victories spreads, it might prompt a tribe somewhere to rebel themselves. Then the shamans won't have just us to worry about, and that will divide their attention and resources."

"Good point," he agreed.

They discussed the matter a little more, and eventually it was decided to send out some men, formerly nazram, who had traveled the land before and who might secretly spread word of what was happening. Shulu would have called such messengers agents of influence, and it was chiefly on her teachings that Shar was drawing now. Wars were not won by battle, but by strategies and tactics.

"There is this also," Shar told them. "I have decided where to go next, but I want your advice before I commit to that decision. So, tell me what you think."

"If we march swiftly," Nahring said, "we can penetrate deep into the Fields of Rah and head straight for the capital. If that falls to us, the war is over."

The other chiefs debated this, and Shar listened attentively. The plan had great merit, but it made her uncomfortable. She had considered it herself, but decided against it.

"The Nagraks are the largest tribe," Asana argued. "Even by themselves, they outnumber us. It would be a hard fight, even with speed and surprise, to overcome them. And they surely must anticipate such a possibility, so I don't think we can count on surprise at all."

Many of the other chiefs agreed with this, and Nahring acknowledged their arguments.

"There is this also," Shar added. "Winter is coming on, and if we didn't succeed in our attack, we would be stranded on the shelterless plains. Defeated, running low on morale, and exposed to the elements."

"We must keep our supply lines intact," Dakashul suggested. "We could head a little south until we come to the Eagle Claw Mountains, and from there conquer the tribes between the Nagraks on the Fields of Rah and the Sun Lo River. That way we could encircle the capital, and find shelter from the bitter winds in the foothills to the mountains or the forests along the river. Come spring, we could then press forward against the capital from several directions at once."

Again, Shar had considered and discarded this, and Kubodin voiced her own reasoning.

"Our forces would have some shelter from the worst of the weather, but they would be stretched out. The enemy might attack us at some point along that long length, and sever our supply lines leaving the head of the army without food, unable to retreat and not at full strength."

The chiefs agreed, and then Argash spoke. "That only leaves heading north. We could make for the Forest of Dreams. It would provide shelter from the weather, and food as well. At least, game would help if our supply lines were severed. But ultimately, going north faces similar risks as going south. Perhaps we should make Tsarin Fen our base. At least from there we could ensure the enemy did not get behind us."

Shar had thought of that too. "You're right. Northward is ultimately as dangerous as southward. Tsarin Fen is the safest of all these options. And yet it takes us no farther into enemy territory than we are already. It does not advance the war. It's also the most likely option for us to take, apart from striking directly toward Nagrak City, so they'll be expecting it."

The smoke from the fire swirled around them, eddying with some current of the air.

"What's your suggestion, then?" Asana asked.

Shar looked at him, and saw that Kubodin exchanged a glance with him as well. She realized they both knew what her idea was, which was not so surprising. They understood both strategy, and her own particular preferences very well.

"I suggest going north, but not to the Forest of Dreams. I suggest Chatchek Fortress."

She could see by the looks on many faces that they did not like it.

"A name of ill omen," Nahring said. "It's said to be haunted."

"It is," Shar confirmed. "I know because I have been there with Asana and Kubodin. I have made peace with the restless spirits though. If they yet remain, they'll do us no harm. And having been there, I also know the advantages the fortress offers. Firstly, from there we can be sure of our supply line. We merely need shift it to a more northern route. In occupying it, we can extend the territory we control, and yet still offer the full army's protection to our incoming supplies. Not only that, it's huge. It's old and damaged, but for the most part we can repair that fairly easily. Then the enemy can attack, if they wish, during the winter. We'll be warm and secure while they're exposed to the elements. They would expend their lives to take such a fortress like grain falling beneath the scythe."

The chiefs did not seem enthusiastic, and she knew why.

"I know it's not the manner in which the Cheng conduct battles," she said. "We're used now to raids and skirmishes. We fight, and the fight is done. We don't use fortresses and siege tactics. Yet our ancestors did. They conducted *war*, while we only conduct *battles*. There is a difference, and if we can recapture the skills of our ancestors faster than the shamans, it's an advantage we have over them."

The chiefs better liked that. They liked to think of themselves as the successors of their ancestors, but Shar knew better than most that they had fallen a long way since the empire of old. Only in Nagrak City was the splendor preserved. At least so Shulu had taught her.

Asana and Kubodin immediately grasped the advantages that she had outlined, and they supported her. After that, the rest agreed, if more so because the alternatives were worse than anything else. But she knew beyond doubt that the tribes were changing. She had formed an army here that worked together in unison. They were growing. They would change more, and the time would come when they would be grateful to be behind walls. That day would be when they saw the vast numbers of soldiers, greater by far than her own army, that the shamans would gather to hurl against them.

4. A Badge of Honor

At last the army marched again, and Shar breathed a sigh of relief. Her fear had been that while they were delayed, the enemy would advance against them. Yet the reports of her scouts showed no evidence of that. There had been sightings of enemy scouts though.

The enemy was incompetent. Time and again they had proved it. They did not have Shar's training, for who could be a better teacher than Shulu who had lived so long, but had also seen the tactics of the first emperor?

It was an advantage, but it would not last. The shamans had been caught by surprise. At some point, likely sooner rather than later, they would appoint a supreme leader for their forces. That person would have skill and knowledge, and on top of that they would also have far greater numbers. Then the enemy would be truly difficult to overcome.

She led the army westward, passing beyond the borders of Tsarin Fen and reaching into the Fields of Rah. She struck straight toward Nagrak City, and did so at a fast pace. When the chiefs questioned her, she smiled.

"Let them think we're coming for them. Let them gather their forces around the capital. There are certainly scouts who will have seen us and reported our movements. That's all for the good. When they hear otherwise, which they will shortly, it will cause confusion and upset their plans."

"You're a wily one," Argash said.

She winked at him. "I must have learnt it from you."

The next day, Shar ordered a change of direction. Now they struck out to the south as the afternoon waned. They marched until the sun began to die, and then established a camp, guarded by a larger than normal number of sentries.

Night fell, and when the cooking fires had been used for their purpose, and the army fed, they were stoked up and in great quiet the army left them burn while they headed back east a little and then turned sharply to the north. Shar led them, and she set a grueling pace.

As they set out, she called Radatan to her. "Send out every scout. Give them instructions to find every enemy scout, and kill them. If we can, we'll leave here without the enemy knowing we've changed direction."

"It will be done, mistress. There will be ones that left to report home earlier though, and we'll not find them. But I guess you want them to return with misinformation?"

"Exactly."

Radatan carried out her orders, and he left with the scouts himself. It was a difficult task. For the area must be searched thoroughly, and it would take a great deal of time. She knew it was unlikely they would find every enemy scout. No doubt some would escape the search, but if so they would at first think her army had continued to march eastward, but had started before the sun rose. It would take them some time to discover differently, and when they reported to their superiors it would only add to the confusing reports. A skilled enemy would see through all her deceptions quickly, but as yet there was no sign of such a one among her opponents.

Shar led the army through the night, and they stopped at dawn and ate a cold meal so that the smoke of their fires could not be seen. The men did not like it, but they trusted her. She had led them with skill, and so far they not only lived but had won victories against superior numbers. They would follow her anywhere, just at the moment.

The army slept briefly, but by mid-morning they were marching again. If she had been forced to remain stationary before, she made up for it now with haste. Even so, by late that afternoon the enemy was in sight.

Asana saw them first, and he drew attention to them in his calm voice.

"Look westward," he said. "We are watched."

Shar glanced casually in the direction so as to appear unconcerned, and so that she could cover her study of them as though she were merely glancing around out of boredom.

The enemy were a half dozen strong, mounted on shaggy ponies, watching from the crest of a slight hill a good distance away. They were making no attempt to hide themselves.

"Are they scouts?" she asked.

"They look like Nagrak warriors to me," Kubodin said.

"I think so too," Asana agreed.

Shar was in doubt. "But are they Nagraks scouting for the enemy, or are they locals just watching us?"

"Surely they're just locals," Argash said. "No scout would ever let themselves be seen like that."

Shar narrowed her eyes at the riders, trying to see more clearly over the distance.

"True enough. Unless they *wanted* to be seen to lure us into a trap."

Kubodin fingered his brass earring for some moments, then spoke.

"Could be, I guess. I don't think so though. You've changed direction and moved too fast. There's no trap out there. Not yet anyway. They're just warriors from the area round about, and they're keeping an eye on us. They know these lands, and they trust their ponies to get them away from us if we send someone out to attack them. They're just curious, as much as anything."

Shar agreed, and she wondered if she could make use of it. The riders might not be part of any enemy army, but they would certainly be in communication with it, sooner or later.

They marched onward, and Shar sent a warrior to find Radatan if he had returned from his mission last night. As night fell, and the camp was being established the former hunter but now leader of her scouts approached.

"You wanted me, Nakatath?"

"I do. Come sit with me by the fire."

They did so, and Shar offered him wine. It was a luxury to the Cheng, for it had to be imported from other lands. The shamans and chiefs she had overturned had a stock of many good things beside money.

"You saw the Nagrak riders on the hill a little while ago?"

"I did. I sent out scouts to see what they do overnight."

"Good. But I have a plan. I'm going to send out a column of three hundred riders first thing tomorrow."

He frowned at that. "That's pretty much all your cavalry. And no disrespect to them, they won't be a match for Nagraks. The Nagraks are born to riding like no other tribe in all the lands of the Cheng."

"Good. You tell me the truth, and I like that. I'm not sending the column out to fight Nagraks though."

He tilted his head a little to the side. "Then why send them?"

"I'm sending them out to *look* like we're trying to pick a fight with the Nagraks. It all adds to the confusion. I don't want the enemy to know where I'm going. Hopefully, I can make them think this is a probe toward Nagrak City to measure resistance. It will also provide a base camp to allow the scouts to extend out farther toward the city as well. Both things may lead our enemies into thinking an attack is imminent."

Radatan considered things for a moment. "It might well work. At the least, it will give them doubt. First, they think you're heading south. Then north. Then maybe striking toward Nagrak City. They won't know *what* to believe, and while they doubt they may hesitate to act themselves."

Shar smiled, but it was a cold smile that bespoke of ill will to her enemies rather than joy.

Radatan caught some of her mood, and he clenched his fist slowly.

"We'll crush them by the end," he said. "Even if it takes years. Would you like me to lead the column? I could do a good job of that, but I'd rather stay as your guard."

Her smile turned to one of genuine mirth. "I think not. I've seen you ride. No, my friend. Stay by my side as guard, and keep doing what you're doing organizing our scouts. Instead, pick the best man you have for me to lead the column. He must be a good scout, able to read the signs that others might miss. He must be a fine warrior also. Most of all he must be a man of cool courage, for he will be going into enemy territory outnumbered."

Radatan thought for some moments, and she could almost read his thoughts as he considered one man after another.

"I have it," he said at length. "Magrig is the one you want. He's from the Smoking Eyes Tribe. He's young, but he's all the things needed for such a task."

Shar trusted his judgement, but it was well to meet the man on whom she would place such a difficult burden.

"Then fetch him. I would speak to him in person."

Radatan was not gone long before he returned, and he brought a strange looking warrior before her. Magrig was indeed young, but he was obviously no stranger to conflict.

Shar studied him as he executed a graceful bow. His left eye was covered by an eye patch. A scar ran down from his forehead to his cheek, obscured only by the patch. He seemed at ease, not changing his demeanor a whit from what she guessed it to ordinarily be. Only the deep bow showed that he was in the presence of royalty, and now that he straightened he seemed as calm as if he were talking to a fellow warrior.

"Your name is Magrig?"

"It is, emperor-to-be."

"A strange name for a Cheng warrior."

"So it is. The belief among the Smoking Eyes Tribe is that many of our ancestors came from foreign lands. We certainly have some strange traditions, and sometimes the names handed down through generations are unusual."

She noticed that his one good eye was that strange gray color that Nahring also possessed.

"Whatever the case," he went on, his voice taking on a slight edge, "I'm all Cheng now, no matter the name."

"I believe you. And you can do your nation a great service, but it'll be dangerous. Has Radatan told you what I want."

"He has," the young man answered crisply.

"Good. Then I won't hold you up. I'll give orders that the cavalry is under your command for this mission, and let you go. You'll want a good night's rest."

"Thank you," he said.

"Good luck then. Just keep in mind that the army will continue in its current direction. At least we don't anticipate any change. So you'll know where to find us in a few days. Take your time, and go carefully. You'll be out there for several days, and it'll be dangerous. Most of all, make it look like an advance column clearing the way to

Nagrak City. Cause any confusion you can, but on no account engage in any fighting if you can avoid it."

"I'll accomplish all those things, or die trying," he said.

She reached out and shook his hand. "Try not to die. I suspect I'll need you for more missions after this."

The young man bowed and left.

"He *is* young," Shar said to Radatan when Magrig was out of earshot.

"So he is, but I vouch for him. He's one of my best men despite his youth."

"It is done," Shar replied. "I trust your judgment, and meeting him just now I get a sense of something ... different about him. He's one that I'll be watching."

It was not long after that the messenger came. Word of him was brought to Shar, for he sought entrance to the camp via the sentries. This was granted, for he was a lone Nagrak rider.

A guard came with him in case he intended any ill, but he seemed to bear no weapons. Shar could see him as he approached, and whatever had been said to those around him put them on edge. There was a sense of shock on their faces.

The rider came close, surrounded by men, and Shar stood, Radatan and Huigar by her side.

"I have a message for Shar Fei," he said.

"I am she," Shar replied. He had not accorded her any title such as Nakatath, so he was not friendly to her. Yet he had accepted who she was by acknowledging her last name, so he intended no obvious insult either.

"These words were given to me by the shamans," he said. "Not just for you to hear, but for all the land."

"Speak freely," Shar told him. "You are a messenger, and no harm will come to you."

The man dismounted and bowed. Shar sensed Radatan and Huigar tense beside her, but she did not think this man intended any sort of attack.

"You have committed crimes against the Cheng people. Where there was harmony, you have brought war. Where law and order prevailed, you have introduced chaos. You have unlawfully killed shamans and chiefs. For these offences, you will be punished. A reward is offered for anyone who kills you. The bounty on your head is ten thousand gold pieces."

The messenger ceased speaking, and a hush fell over all who could hear. Shar straightened. She had expected retaliation to her letter from the shamans, but this had not been foreseen. For ten thousand in gold, she might even sell herself out. The temptation would be massive for anyone around her. Which was an army of thousands of armed men.

She smiled. "The victor of any war declares the enemy criminals. It has always been thus. The beaten side has no power to defend themselves. So it has been for a thousand years. This is a year of change though. Your message has been delivered, but whether it was delivered to a beaten force, or the victor, whether it will be considered true or laughed at, remains to be seen."

Shar turned to the warriors who had brought the messenger in.

"This man has discharged his duty. Treat him with courtesy, replenish his supplies with whatever he needs, and then escort him through the sentries in safety."

The warriors obeyed, and the messenger said no more, yet he gave a bow before he remounted and was led off.

The army was no longer quiet, but a hiss of whispered conversation filled the area all around Shar. Like a ripple she could sense news of the bounty spreading through the camp.

Kubodin whistled through his teeth. "Ten thousand, hey? At last they give you the respect you deserve."

She laughed at that. "I guess so. I could do without that kind of honor, though."

The chiefs were sent out to talk to the soldiers and gauge how they felt. Shar was worried that the whole army might turn against her, but Asana seemed unconcerned.

"What will be will be," he merely said. And then when pressed, he smiled faintly. "It could work to the disadvantage of the shamans. If they have ten thousand in gold to give to the person who kills you, where does such a vast amount of money come from? It belongs to the people, and they know it. They will also know how much the shamans fear you now."

Radatan and Huigar were far less optimistic. They said nothing, but sat and sharpened their blades in the tent. When they were done with that, they took it in turns to patrol the outside, and set up several braziers all around it so that no one could approach unseen.

She looked at Kubodin, who had been quiet. He seemed to doze in a chair, less concerned even than Asana, but it was hard to tell with him if he really slept or only rested. Either way, his hand lay loosely against the haft of his axe.

It was late into the night before the other chiefs returned, and it did not escape Shar's attention that they returned together. No doubt they had held their own meeting before they saw her. She saw no duplicity in their eyes though when they entered the tent.

"Well then?" she asked. "What's the mood of the camp?"

Nahring flashed her a grin, and those cool gray eyes of his sparkled.

"No doubt there are some who would think of trying to claim the reward. But they won't try. They'd be killed on sight. The rest of the army would turn on them quicker than a wolf jumping a blind deer."

"Are you sure?"

"We're sure," Argash said. "Not only are they not tempted by the gold, the bounty fills them with pride. They call you their *ten-thousand-emperor*, and they say how much the shamans hate you. They see that hatred as a badge of honor, for it means you're beating them."

Shar was amazed by that reaction, and for a moment she felt a sense of being buoyed by the thousands and thousands of Cheng who willed her to success, but Radatan's gruff reply brought her to grim reality again.

"Maybe so. But it still only takes one knife in the dark to kill."

5. Ambush

Magrig knew he was young, but he also knew opportunity when it came and sat down beside him. And this was an opportunity now.

Not only did it sit down beside him, it put wood on the fire and shared a meal with him. If he performed his task with skill, one that had only been given to him because he had somehow impressed Radatan, then all things were possible. He might become…

He stopped that train of thought. He would be nothing unless he succeeded, and he must focus all his intention on that. Time enough to take advantage of the good fortune that had befallen him later. If he were still alive.

The empress-to-be had warned him. This mission was dangerous. Not only that, but important. No matter his personal fate, if his column of riders failed then the army that fought for the freedom of the Cheng nation would be in greater jeopardy. There was no doubt that Shar was a shrewd commander. Her victories so far had been despite inferior numbers. What he did now was a kind of game. He must send a message to the shamans, and he must make them believe it no matter that it was deception. He did not know what Shar's final gambit was, nor did he need to know. He knew that this would buy her time, or give her some advantage, and it was his job to make it happen.

He would sooner sit beside a fire with a pack of starving dogs than fail the mission Shar had given him. No matter the cost, he vowed he would *not* fail.

The sun was just now rising, casting its spears of light over the grasslands, but he and his column were already riding and a mile from the camp.

He glanced at Gnarhash, the Iron Dog scout who he had chosen as his second in command. Neither of them were great riders, and both would prefer to be on foot, but the mission required cavalry.

"Keep your eyes open," he said. "We're in Nagrak land now, and I don't want any surprises."

"There's nothing to see." Gnarhash was not a man given to long conversations, which was one of his better qualities. He was a good scout too, and a handy man in a fight.

Magrig gazed out over the empty-looking grasslands, turning from left to right slowly.

"That's what worries me. There are gulleys through these plains, and patches of tall grass. It's said that Nagrak riders can hide perfectly in both and launch a surprise attack from no more than fifty feet away."

The other man gave no reply, but Magrig could tell by his casual, if frequent, glances all around them that he took the danger seriously.

The column wound onward, and they made good time. Magrig decided to set a stiff pace, but not one so fast that it would tire the horses. They might need them yet to get out of trouble. Three hundred was a strong force, but the Nagraks were a massive tribe. He did not think any of the local villages could muster anywhere near that many riders against him. Nor did he think the enemy army, if a second one had yet even been formed, was nearby. He did not *know* either of those things though. Making assumptions was the sort of thing that got a man killed. He had nearly died once. He did not wish to go through that again.

He lifted the eyepatch a little to scratch the skin beneath in the socket. He was careful that no one saw this.

It unnerved some of the men, but he was used to the loss now. He was not quite as good a fighter as before, for his judgment of how far away a blade was had deteriorated, but he was still good. Most of all, he was smarter. Near-death experiences had that influence on a man. He would survive this mission, and prosper from it.

They rode through the day, and afternoon rolled over the land. It was not like his home. It was wide and open. It was silent too. He heard nothing save the breeze stirring the tall grasses, and the constant rumble of three hundred horses moving at a trot.

It was too quiet. He called the column to a halt, and they rested. He did not like this. Where was the enemy? Surely they knew he was here now. There was no sign of them though. No scouts. No riders in the distance. Nothing.

They had come to a narrow track. It could not be called a road, yet wherever people passed in numbers large enough to kill grass and tramp down the earth to hardened dust, there must be a destination in mind. That meant a village.

The track headed roughly south and north. He chose southward, and when their break was done headed down it. There would only be one more spell of riding before dusk signaled it was time to establish a camp.

Gnarhash nudged his mount, a shaggy pony that had a bad habit of biting, level with him.

"Sir? If we keep going this way we'll surely find a village. That might mean fighting."

"Somehow, I don't think so."

"What do you mean?"

Magrig kept his voice down so the next riders in the column could not hear him.

"I don't think anyone will be there. They know we're here, but we haven't seen so much as a shepherd boy. Even their flocks must be in hiding. And that worries me."

Gnarhash said nothing for a little while, thinking things through slowly but surely as he was want to do.

"You fear they're setting us up so we'll lower our guard. Then they'll ambush us."

There was no need to answer. They both knew that was a possibility, and the more abandoned the land seemed to be, the more it seemed like a trap.

They came to the village as the setting sun blushed the sky pink. It was medium sized, containing dozens of huts, none of which produced any smoke from the hearths within them that should have been cooking dinner. It seemed empty otherwise too.

Magrig signaled ten riders to split off from the column to go and investigate. It was close to dark before they returned.

"There's no one there," said one of the men. It was Damril from the Green Hornet Tribe, and Magrig was watching him. He showed signs of talent.

Magrig maneuvered his horse around to face the column.

"Men! Courtesy of the enemy, we'll have roofs over our heads tonight, and maybe even some firewood already gathered for us. Rest easy tonight, but on no account eat any food left behind or drink water from any well. It may be poisoned."

He turned to Gnarhash. "Establish two lines of sentries. And have scouts sent out several miles in all directions."

Gnarhash went to arrange that, and he did not even look surprised. He feared a trap too, but the chance to sleep under cover was too good to pass up. The men would rest better, and he needed to keep them fresh.

Anything was possible tomorrow. The deeper they went into the Fields of Rah, the more dangerous it would get.

The night was passed peacefully, and next morning Magrig set himself for the next task required. He did not wish to do it, yet it must be done.

They mounted, and he called Gnarhash over. "Get a few men to set fire to the huts."

He led the men westward, deeper into Nagrak territory, and a plume of smoke rose high behind them in the still air. Far up, it met a layer of different air that drifted north, and the smoke bent in that direction. Magrig wished he could go that way too. By tonight, he would have gone as far as he dared into enemy land and would then be able to strike out to the north as well.

Gnarhash caught his attention. "Many of the men aren't happy at firing the huts."

It was not hard to see why. They themselves, whatever tribe they were from, lived in huts like that too. For many of them, it was all they had, simple as it was. They did not like to see such things destroyed, for they knew the hardship it would cause.

"Spread word among them that I wish it were otherwise. But that smoke will be seen from far, far away. It will lead our opponents into thinking we bring war to them, but it's a deception. We don't. Nakatath is working to another plan, and if we can deceive them now we can save more lives later."

He was not sure what the plan was, or where they were going except that it was to the north. If he succeeded in this mission, he might by so proving himself be allowed deeper into her policies.

They passed other villages during the day, and they were empty like the last had been. These too he burned, and there was a haze of smoke filling the air behind them. No matter that this land seemed abandoned he knew it was not. There were eyes out there somewhere, and messages would be sent back to Nagrak City, or to an army if one was marching toward them.

He rested the column a little before dusk, making it seem to any who watched from a distance that they were establishing another camp. However, learning from what Shar had done, this was not his attention at all. He had sent word for the men to eat cold rations, and to be ready for a night ride.

When it was dark, he moved ahead half a mile, then veered directly north. Risking injury in the dim conditions, he set a sharp pace. He wanted as much ground as possible between where he was last seen and where he ended up. The growing fear of an enemy attack motivated him. No Cheng warrior willingly endured their tribal lands being invaded. There were Nagraks out there somewhere, and they intended the column harm. It was only a matter of when, and how they would strike.

They rested at intervals through the night, and took one long break after midnight where the horses were well rested and the men caught a little sleep. They grumbled at this, but not a lot. They too felt the eerie silence of the land, and their eyes were constantly straining against the dark in fear of an attack.

They were riding as the dawn came, and by its light were relieved that no enemy riders were seen behind them. If an attack had been planned on their camp last night, they had eluded it.

"Time to turn back to our army," Magrig said to Gnarhash. His second in charge said nothing, but there was the slightest expression of relief on his face.

The country they rode through was changing. The grass was less lush, and there were no trees at all. It was a barren wasteland, at least by the normal standards of the Fields of Rah. All the better to avoid the enemy, but there were folds and undulations. It might have been dry now, but in times of heavy rain many of these shallow channels and gulleys would fill quickly with water and make swift travel impossible. He glanced to the sky, but it was clear and promised only good weather.

They pressed on. The mood of the men brightened, for they were heading back toward Shar now. It was in her that they trusted, and it was in her that they believed. She had come from nowhere like a fire among them, and she had set their hearts ablaze with her beauty, and even more so with the skill that she used to humble the shamans.

Magrig felt the pull Shar exerted. There was something about her that was special. For him, it was her courage, for truly what she did was bold, and the consequences of failure could be worse than death. If the shamans captured her, the fate she must suffer would be terrible. Better by far if some assassin killed her, but that would not be easy. She was a fighter such as he had rarely ever seen, and she had the use of magic swords. So maybe, just maybe, she might endure all her trials and prevail in the end. He hoped so. Not just for the Cheng nation, but himself. If she fell, those who supported her must fall also.

He brought his mind back to the task at hand. The column now headed away from danger, but they were not out of it yet. They would not be safe until they rejoined Shar's army.

Ahead was a gulley running a half mile or longer across their route, far larger than most they had seen. Likewise, it was filled with shrubbery and trees. He did not like the look of it. In such a place men could set an ambush.

He drew the column to a halt. "What do you think, Gnarhash? Send scouts down first, and if it's clear, cross it? Or circle around?"

His second in charge raised a hand over his eyes to protect them from the morning glare, and studied the terrain.

"Use the scouts. But don't cross until they've checked a fair way in each direction."

It seemed good advice to Magrig. "Pick a few men, and give the orders then."

"I see movement!" yelled one of the riders farther back down the column. Then there were other shouts. A moment later Nagrak riders burst up over the banks of the gulley and rolled toward them like seething flood water.

Magrig summed up the situation with a glance. An ambush had been placed here, but it was a smaller force of only a hundred. No doubt the enemy had planned for more, but could not get enough horsemen here in time because of the way he had swiftly changed direction. He could try to outgallop them, but they were the best riders in the land. That was futile. Worse, doing so might see them herded toward another force of the enemy that might be approaching. There was only one thing to do.

"Quickly!" he cried to Gnarhash. "Signal a charge!"

His second in command lifted a horn hanging around his neck, and blew a hurried but piercing note. The column formed into a wedge shape, with Magrig at its point, then kicked their horses into a gallop and drew their sabers.

The two forces met in a thunder of hooves, and Magrig slashed out at a Nagrak rider who cut at him at the same time. Their swords met in a clash of steel, and all around them the screech of metal against metal, the cries of men and the squeals of horses rent the air.

His opponent's blade nearly broke past his own defenses, but then their mounts moved farther apart and Magrig was able to send a faster backhanded cut at the Nagrak rider than the other was able to do at him. The point of his blade nicked his enemy's throat and red blood swelled to the spot. Then they were past each other, and Magrig did not know if it had been a killing blow or not. Nor did it matter. Another enemy was before him.

The next few moments were a red blur as both forces sought to destroy the other. Yet like a sudden storm had passed and the clouds rolled back to reveal a blue sky again, the charge carried the column through the enemy to the other side.

Magrig swung around, and looked for Gnarhash to give the order to turn and charge again, but all he saw was the mount of his second in charge, its saddle empty.

He took his own horn in trembling hands that were spattered in blood that he did not think was his own, but did not blow it. There was no need for another charge. The enemy had not had time to prepare the ambush properly, and it was a smaller force. Most of them lay dead on the trodden ground. Perhaps a dozen were racing away to the west, though one of those looked injured and likely to fall. His swift action in charging had caught them unprepared.

His riders swung up around him, and he could see the column was still intact, though they must have lost at least twenty men. Gnarhash was among them, and Magrig saw him now, his saber still in his hand but his head half cut away where he lay on the battle-churned ground.

Magrig studied his men a moment, and saw the Green Hornet warrior Damril close by.

"You," Magrig said. "You just got a promotion. Pick five men and search the battlefield. Kill any of the enemy who live, and see if any of ours do. Then quickly catch any mounts you can. Shar needs more horses."

Damril wasted no time following his orders, and Magrig went among the rest of the riders checking on the wounded and helping bandage cuts and slashes as best he could. Another two men died, but the rest seemed fit to ride.

They gathered together swiftly again, and Magrig sent several riders down the gulley to scout it. He thought the ambush had been sprung already, but caution dictated he checked.

It was not long before they returned. "It's clear, sir."

He ordered the men onward, but he hung back himself. He gazed at the horizon, scrutinizing it for any sign of the enemy. He knew they were there. Like a cat hidden in a shrub waiting for pigeons in a tree to land near it. They were out there, somewhere. Probably closer than he thought.

With a nudge of his heels he finally urged his mount forward. His gaze lingered a final time on Gnarhash. The man was unlucky. A bright future had been ahead of him, but now there was nothing. War had stolen it from him, and the ill chances of the world.

Magrig passed through the gulley, and came up to the front of the men at the other side.

"You fought well, lads," he told them. "I'll see Nakatath knows it. Our mission is accomplished. We made it look like Shar's army was testing the Nagrak borders, and that will confuse them. They won't know what she plans or where she'll strike next. Be assured, if we can't guess what she's up to, the enemy can't. In the meantime, keep your eyes open. I mistrust the riders who got away. I think they know help is close by, and that's bad news for us. We're not safe yet, so don't let your guard down for a moment."

He gestured for Damril to lead them on at a trot. The men had to get used to his increased authority. Magrig just hoped he had more luck as second in charge than Gnarhash had.

They moved across the plains at a good pace, and they saw no sign of Nagrak riders. Yet Magrig did see eagles circling in the sky. Coincidence maybe, or perhaps as legend said, the eyes of the shamans. Whatever the case, he decided they would camp early this afternoon, and thenceforward travel only at night until he rendezvoused with Shar.

6. I Must Do It

The days passed uneasily for Shar. She worried about Magrig and his men. She had sent them into danger. So too she was worried that she had committed the bulk of her cavalry, such as it was, to the venture. It was a great risk, even if lessened somewhat by her intent to occupy a fortress rather than roam the land. Worst of all was the eagles though.

They had appeared not long after the messenger that told of the bounty on her head. That the shamans used the birds as their eyes, she did not doubt. Her enemy knew where she was, despite all her attempts at misdirection. Yet they were not futile. Though they knew where she was, they could not guess what she intended to do. She might yet strike toward Nagrak City. Or venture north in an encircling maneuver and try to bring more tribes to her cause. Let the enemy debate those choices. Neither was her intention.

She was satisfied with the plan to refortify Chatchek. It would work to her advantage, not least because it was not the Cheng way of fighting. It would be unanticipated. But coming north might solve the worst problem of all, which was her lack of defense against sorcerous attack. Of her plan for that, the chiefs knew nothing as yet. It was time that they did though, even if they would not like it.

The eagles worried her. Not just that they knew where the army was, but that they might study it and learn more of the way she organized it than she would like. They would come to know in which tent she slept, who her messengers were, and any details that might help an assassin. To counter this, at least partially, she had given the order that they would march only at night.

The scouts were pushed hard. It might be catastrophic if Shar's army marched into a trap, and this was easier set at night. To that end, the scouts ranged less distance from the army than usual, but covered the ground ahead, both day and night, with great care.

Asana was walking beside her one night. "Magrig has been gone a few days now. I hope all is well, but he's due back."

"There was something about him," Shar replied. "I'm not sure what it was. Call it determination. I don't doubt he's run into trouble, but he's the sort of man who can handle it."

Dawn came, and they established a camp. Shar went into her tent before the light could reveal her to eagles, and she summoned the chiefs to her for a meeting. Such a thing might pinpoint her tent, but she had taken care to ensure that all the chiefs had guards in front of their tents, just like hers, and that the chiefs wore hoods when they moved around from tent to tent, as did she, and that they never met in the same tent twice in a row.

They entered, and they sat around a brazier while food was brought to them. They ate with relish, for a night march in the cooler air produced a sharper hunger, and when they were done she broached the subject that had been on her mind incessantly since the last battle.

"Gentlemen, you know as well as I do that the sorcery of the shamans is our greatest threat. Against all tradition, and against the morals of the people, they've employed it in battle."

"It's a dire threat," Kubodin said. "And it'll help them in the short term, but it's a risky gamble. If you survive for any length of time, and you will, their influence over the people will wane. Already they're disliked, but to kill warriors with magic is a thing few warriors will support, no matter who they fight for. The longer you endure, the more tribes will come to your side because they will see that you truly are a better alternative to the rule of the shamans."

Shar knew that was true, but she was not so certain as he that she would endure. As Radatan had put it, all it took was one knife in the dark and all was over.

"Maybe so," she answered, "but I have found a means to do more than endure. It's one that I've long thought of, though Shulu warned me against it. The peril is near as great as the shamans. Yet it offers a means to fight back against them, magic for magic."

The other chiefs leaned in, all attention to what she would propose. On many faces she saw curiosity, on some, who belonged to her friends, concern.

"What means is this?" Dakashul asked.

"Of old," Shar told them, "my great forefather faced the same problem I face now. He had Shulu with him, and she was younger and stronger than now. Yet by herself she was not enough. It's hard for the one to prevail against many. So, between them, they coaxed, persuaded and appealed to a faction of the shamans that were not as the rest. They were ones that had sympathy for Shulu's views that the shamans had transgressed their power. They had moved from advisors to the people to *rulers* of the people. Anyway, eventually they won those shamans over and fifty of them joined forces with the emperor and fought for him against their own order."

The chiefs seemed puzzled. "I've never heard those stories," Argash said.

"No. But I heard them from Shulu. It was earlier in the war against the shamans, and the plan failed. The shamans ended up betraying the emperor, and they in turn were defeated by Shulu and their memory erased. It was a failure of the emperor, and those things tended to be hidden. So their aid, and their betrayal, was buried and forgotten. But Shulu remembered."

Shar studied the chiefs. They looked thoughtful, as well they should be. History was a concoction of the powerful, and the truth was often hidden, obscured, or turned into a lie. Of them all, Asana looked the most thoughtful. He was more learned than the rest, and it might be that he had once read or heard something that touched on the issue.

As always though, it was Kubodin who got straight to the point.

"How does this help us?"

There it was. The crux of the matter, and Shar knew no one would like what she had to say next, but fate had forced her into the situation.

"The shamans who served the emperor betrayed him, and I said they were defeated. I did not say they were killed. Instead, they were imprisoned. Shulu tricked them, for even she could not stand against fifty. They were caught in a trap of magic, and confined in a valley not that far from here. They cannot escape. Yet I know how to release them, and I think they'll serve me."

Straightaway there was a tumult of voices, and Huigar and Radatan stuck their heads through the entrance to make sure all was well. She waved to them that all was fine, and the chiefs slowly subsided.

"That was a thousand years ago," Argash said. "Surely they would all be dead by now?"

"Perhaps," Shar agreed. "But Shulu did not think so. The allies she and the emperor chose were powerful, and many of them knew the secret longevity magic that the shamans possess. Through that alone, they might live. There is an even better reason to expect them to still be alive though."

"What's that?" Nahring asked.

"Shulu caught them in a trap, and though she did not trust them any longer, still she thought they might be needed, and might yet be brought back and persuaded to serve the emperor. So the trap was a great magic. Highest of the high, and beyond the knowledge of the shamans to break out from, or other shamans to free them from outside. She caught them in a moment of time. Even as time flows forward for everyone as a river, so too, just like a river, sometimes a stagnant backwater forms. It's part of the river, but doesn't flow with it. At least, that's how Shulu explained it to me. So for them, time has not passed as swiftly as for the rest of the world. And she told me how I can release the trap, if in great need."

Kubodin whistled. "That truly is a great magic."

The other chiefs seemed impressed, as well they should be. Shulu was the greatest shaman in the land, and Shar only needed to feel the Swords of Dawn and Dusk in her hands to be reminded of it.

Asana glanced at her, and she read the doubt on his face.

"It seems to me," the swordmaster said, "that these shamans, no matter that they disagree with their own kind, betrayed your forefather. So they are not to be trusted. Worse than that, he and Shulu trapped them. So they will have no love for you. The emperor and Shulu aren't here, so their hatred, which they have had a long time to whet in lonely bitterness, will be sharp as a dagger and they will aim it at your heart."

His fear was the same fear that Shulu had expressed when they discussed the possibility of freeing them. Back then, such conversations were like games. *If the shamans did this, what would you do? If such and such happened, how would you respond?* It was a good way of training, and the scenarios were endless. She had discovered now though that playing out scenarios like that was easy. Real life was infinitely harder, and nothing had happened in reality the way those games unfolded. Still, it had taught her to think, to weigh up possibilities, to balance risk against potential gain.

"All you say is true, but the overriding idea is that those shamans are *needed*. Shulu didn't think our enemies would use sorcery against warriors. So we *must* have protection, or all our gains will be lost, and the Cheng nation will fall back into servitude."

There was a deep silence then, and Shar spoke into it. If the chiefs were unhappy, it was about to become worse.

"I told you that I have the knowledge to release the trap in which the shamans are caught. If I could, I'd charge another to accomplish that task, and give to them the means of doing it. That isn't how the trap works though. I have to be there myself." She chose her words carefully now, for on the chance that any of these men betrayed her she did not wish the enemy to learn anything of Shulu's magic. "Only I can release it. Only a descendant of the emperor has the power. So I must go, and I cannot risk taking the army with me. I've already brought the army as close to the trap as I dare. If the enemy sends their army against us, I'll be cut off from reaching it. So I must go alone, while my army draws any opposition away from my true goal."

Where there was a deep silence before, now the chiefs broke into uproar. Argash was the loudest of them.

"Shar! You can't do this. If you're killed, all is lost. Maybe it is without the help of shamans, and maybe not. But without you, there's *nothing*."

She expected that, and had a plan to help ease them into the idea.

"I have to go, my friend. There's just no other way. I will, if you all insist, take a few people with me for protection. Just a few though. Any more, and we'll certainly be observed and in greater danger than if I went alone."

Kubodin gripped his axe. "I'll go," he said.

"As will I," Asana added.

This, she had anticipated. True friends as these were rare, and if she had to go into danger it would be with such as they.

"Alas," she replied. "In my absence, someone must lead the army. You both could do that, as could all the chiefs, but only you, Kubodin, possess magic. Whomever leads might need that, for our enemy may send sorcery against them. So you must take charge, both because you can and because you have the best chance of surviving a scheme of the shamans. Otherwise, I would take you."

Kubodin looked indecisive, which was a countenance so rarely seen on him that she was surprised. She knew his thoughts though. His loyalty was to her first, before the army. He could not say that in hearing of the other chiefs though, and he understood the logic of her decision. He was trying to find a way around it, but such a way did not exist. If it did, she would have found it during the sleepless nights while she had wrestled with the choice herself.

She reached out and placed a hand on his. "Rest easy, I *will* return."

She glanced at Asana. "Your offer I can accept, and in your company I shall feel as safe as though a hundred warriors came to guard me. Radatan and Huigar, who guard this tent even as we speak, just as they guard me every day, have just before agreed to come as well. Gentlemen, I shall be safe. I shall succeed in my mission, and I shall return to the army with the help we must have."

They still did not like it. But no more than Kubodin could find a different path through the situation, neither could they. This was the only way forward, and all else substituted the pretense of safety in the short term for the certainty of failure in the end. She did not fool herself though. Despite her words, the peril of what she was going to undertake was great. She tried to give them the confidence of success she lacked herself.

Argash got down on his knee, and he looked at her with pleading eyes.

"Shar, I beg you not to risk this. Let me go in your place, or if that cannot be done, take the army with you. The Cheng nation cannot afford to lose you. You are everything to us."

7. Give Me Your Word

Shar was touched. Argash had always been close, yet she had kept her secrets from him. He harbored no resentment at that though, as he might have done.

"I'm sorry, my old friend. It must be this way. I think not just of myself, nor my friends. For the Cheng nation we must all make sacrifices, and this is one of them. The risk must be taken."

There was a challenge outside then, and Shar heard Radatan ask a question. She heard little of the answer, but with relief she caught Magrig's name. At last, he had returned.

Huigar announced him, and held open the tent flap for him to walk through. Shar saw instantly that he had suffered a hard time of things. He looked deadly tired, and there was dried blood on his clothes. Even so, he entered with grace and offered polite greetings to everyone gathered.

Shar offered him a chair, and served him a goblet of wine by her own hand. He was calm, yet there was a feverish look to his one eye that spoke of remembered hardship.

"The mission was successful," he said, sipping delicately at his wine. "We went quite deep into the Fields of Rah. The villages we came across were abandoned. Some of these we fired, and it surely must have seemed that we were an advance column of your army. We had trouble getting out though."

Shar had thought as much. "You were forced into battle?"

"Yes."

"How much of the cavalry survived?" She asked the question with dread. She had been lucky in her campaign so far, but her good luck could not continue.

"It was a close thing, but we escaped an ambush intact, with the loss of twenty men. We lost another ten in skirmishes thereafter. I estimate casualties among the enemy to be one hundred and fifty."

Shar studied him carefully. She did not think he was lying. He did not look that type of man, and the truth would come out from the cavalry anyway. She had expected more losses than that.

She topped up his goblet. "You did well, Magrig. Very well indeed. It's imperative that we keep the enemy guessing as to our intentions. Every day that we can achieve that is a victory to us."

He then explained in greater detail all that had happened, and Shar's respect for him grew. Time and again he had trod the narrow path to success, and it had not been easy in enemy lands among those who were better riders. Yet all the time he gave credit to the cavalry and their courage rather than his decisions.

She sent him to get some well-earned rest then, but as he was leaving for the first time he showed a hint of being pleased with his actions.

"One more thing. This is no substitute for saving the lives of warriors, but we did capture ponies in that first battle and the skirmishes afterward."

"How many?"

"One hundred and thirteen."

Shar flashed him her best grin. "Remarkable. Now, get some sleep. You'll need rest. Tomorrow, you take up duties as head of our cavalry. Our growing cavalry, thanks to you."

He bowed and left, and Shar considered the news he had brought. The mission had been successful, and she was now gaining the beginning of a proper cavalry force. It would not help her at Chatchek, but who knew how valuable such an asset might be in the future?

She addressed the chiefs. "Things begin to fall into place, gentlemen. I'll not be gone on my mission long. While I'm away, Kubodin will lead you. His word will be as my word. Tell me you will follow him. Give me your promise."

This was something she had worried about. Chiefs were independent and competitive with other chiefs, and they would not like one of their own put above them. Yet it was Kubodin, a man they all admired, and who possessed his great axe, the only talisman among them all that could protect against magic.

They gave their undertakings, and they did so willingly enough, or seemed to. She did not think there would be problems. At least, so long as she returned to them. If not, then eventually the army would fall apart.

"There's something you can do while I'm gone. You will know who among your men is suitable for this. Find a dozen or so between you all, and give them this task. Go forth among the Cheng and spread news of our victories. This will be dangerous for them, so they must do it in secret. If they're discovered by the shamans, they'll be killed. Tell them to find those who are sympathetic to our cause. Let them judge that carefully, for their lives depend on getting it right. Spread that word, and tell those who receive it to spread it also. That way we can help plant the seeds of rebellion. When we have more victories against the enemy, that seed will grow, and maybe take root by itself. The shamans might find themselves beset from several directions at once."

"It might be hard to find warriors willing to do that," Dakashul said. "Most would prefer the simplicity of fighting with swords, and they might fear being called cowards for leaving the army when there are battles yet to come."

Shar considered that. "Maybe so, but find what men you can. Tell them that what they do will take courage, and that it will strike a blow at the enemy greater than any sword can do."

8. The Cover of Night

That night, soon after the army commenced to march and without ceremony, Shar and her small group of companions slipped away on their quest.

Only Kubodin accompanied them, walking with the travelers past the sentries. They all wore their hoods up so that they would not be recognized, but Kubodin carried a torch and ensured his face could be seen so that no questions were asked.

The little man shook their hands one by one, and wished them luck. He shared a joke with Asana, covering his fear for his friend with humor as he so often did. Yet when he came to Shar, words failed him and he hugged her instead.

Shar was surprised, for he rarely showed this side to his nature no matter that it was always there.

"Take care, Shar. I trust no shamans, no matter if they're a rebel group or not. They betrayed your forefather, so never take your eyes off them. Especially if they agree to help."

"I will, Kubi."

He smiled at the use of that name of affection, but glanced at Radatan and Huigar. They pretended not to have noticed, and the little warrior saluted her and began to turn away to leave.

"You be careful too, old friend," she said to him. "You're in as much danger as I am. If you can get to Chatchek safely though, refortify it, and man the walls you'll be safe for a good while. Wait for me there, but if I don't return it will fall to you to at least try to keep the rebellion alive."

They parted then, and the night swallowed them. It took Shar back to her earlier days in Tsarin Fen, when it was just her, or maybe her and a few scouts, alone in the wild. This was where she was comfortable rather than leading an army, constantly surrounded by noise and conversation. This was her home, as living among a large group of people never would be.

It was a dark night, and the air cooled swiftly. Dew formed on the grass, and their boots became wet. She did not mind. This was magic. The shamans could keep their spells, for no enchantment was greater than walking through the night shadows, breathing the wine-like air that intoxicated with life, and seeing the landscape by the faint shimmer of starlight that crowned the heavens with glory.

They made good time, and they spoke but seldom. Shar led them, for she knew where they were going, and she reveled in taking the front rather than being guarded at the rear. Radatan and Huigar had not liked it at first, but Asana had only smiled. Besides, she was as good a scout, or better, than they were. It was safer this way.

There was a risk of discovery by enemy scouts, or even running into scouts from her own army. The further they traveled though the less risk of this there was. By midnight, Shar thought the chances of any such meeting was extremely unlikely. They rested and spoke softly, but lit no fire.

"How far away is this trap the shamans were caught in?" Asana asked.

"Not far," she replied. "A few more days away, or nights as the case may be. I think it'll be safer to travel that way."

They moved on soon after. In the distance a pack of wolves began to howl, and frogs croaked close by to their left in what must be some lower lying land. Shar veered away from it. If the ground became damp they would leave tracks and she was being careful to keep any signs of their passing as small as possible. She did not want any curious scouts, or worse, a group of Nagrak riders getting curious and following them.

The night grew old, and they traveled through it resting often but only for short spells. Shar drew her cloak tightly about her, and for much of the time kept her hood up. The air held a chill, and whispered of winter. Often though, she pulled the hood down and listened. The cloth kept her warmer, but it hindered hearing.

There was no sign of anyone though. They were in the wilderness by themselves, yet she still changed course at times, veering right or left so as not to be predicable and to give her a chance to pause and watch their backtrail in case they were pursued.

There was no indication of that though, and for a scout to follow them at night they would have to stay close and be greatly skilled.

In the east, the sky grayed. Dawn was approaching, and in the hollows they traversed at times the dew had turned to frost. She felt more confident that her plan of slipping away at night had worked. Likewise, in case there were any spies in her army, which there certainly were, no announcement of her departure would be given for a few days. And when it was announced, the men would be told simply that she had gone away on a task that only she could do, and would rejoin them shortly. Every day she was away though the army would grow more restless.

Just before it was light they stopped and established a camp in one of the many hollows scattered over this part of the plain. It was cold within it, but it offered the protection of shrubbery so they could not be seen, and a small tree at its rim that offered concealment for a lookout to monitor the surrounding lands during the day.

They had not brought a lot in the way of supplies, preferring to travel swiftly and hoping to rejoin the army soon, but they unshouldered their packs and ate a breakfast of dried meat and hard cheese that had come from Tsarin Fen.

"We've covered a lot of ground," Huigar said. The Smoking Eyes tribeswoman sat cross-legged and drew her sword after eating, which she commenced to sharpen with a small whetstone. It did not need it, for it had not been used all night. Even so, Shar understood. A good sword might mean the difference between life and death, and a good warrior cared for it daily. Just in the same way a cavalry rider loved their horse and ensured it was fed, watered and looked after before they tended to their own needs.

"We still have a good way to go, though," Shar replied.

Asana, who was sitting cross-legged as well, yet with his head bowed as though sleeping, lifted it and looked straight at Shar.

"Where, exactly, are we going? I notice you didn't tell the chiefs this."

Shar had drawn her own swords, but she merely inspected them. She had long since discovered that the magic inside them prevented them from blunting, and no whetstone had ever made the slightest impression upon the metal.

"It was no accident that I didn't tell them. It's not that I don't trust them, but what they don't know they can't reveal by accident to a spy."

"Will you tell us, then?"

"Of course. There's more to the story than what I told the others. Listen closely now, and I'll tell you what Shulu told me."

They drew in closer, their attention on her. Shar was so used to secrecy all her life that she found it hard to reveal all that she knew, but these were her friends, and she was learning how to treat them as such.

9. Divide the Enemy's Power

Shulu Gan, once-leader of the shamans, founder of their order, but now outcast, raised her head from the log on which she rode down the stream.

She was tired and wet, and the fever that had made her ill still lingered in her aching joints. Or maybe that was just old age. Her clothes were sodden, and she shivered with cold.

The log had slowed of late. And this stretch of the river was wider but gentler than others. The Forest of Dreams was well behind her now, and it was time to gain the bank and dry out. Much longer of this, and the fever would come back on her, and she might not survive it the second time around.

It was not easy, but she managed to change the direction of the log and swing it toward the bank. The current was sluggish now, and it took time, but eventually it shuddered into an area that seemed part water, part mud and part grass. Nearly, it overturned on her, but she scrambled away from it in time.

She clambered up the bank, falling back once or twice, then finally gained dry ground and threw herself down on the grass. There she lay panting, and let the morning sun play over her.

It was tempting to drift off to sleep. She was tired, and the sun was beautiful, but she mistrusted her situation. Something had stalked her in the forest, and though she had escaped it a wise person took few chances. She lifted herself up on one elbow and looked around.

The forest was a smudge on the horizon to her north. Around her were open grasslands, with here and there a stand of trees.

Her body ached in protest, but she came to her feet and started walking toward the nearest group of trees. Her clothes were still wet, and the sun would take too long to dry them. She needed a fire, and the trees would help scatter the smoke and hide her presence from any eyes on the plains.

It was a stand of elms, tall and stately. There was little undergrowth though, and she knew that cattle, wild or domesticated, grazed here. That meant that a village might be close by, though she could see no sign of it. At any rate, fallen timber was plentiful, and she started a small fire of dry branches with a touch of her hand and a spark of magic.

The fire burned with good heat, once it caught properly. It did not give off much smoke, but what there was she studied as it rose, and noted that the leaf canopy above dispersed it as she had hoped.

She stripped off her wet clothes, and lay them on the ground as close to the flame as she dared. They would dry quickly, but there was no remedy for what ailed her. Old age had no cure. Yet she did feel a little better straight away.

The magic of longevity was always at her disposal, yet even that had failed her of late. Her time on earth was nearly done, and apart from Shar she did not care. The rest from care and the travails of the world would bring her peace. It was rumored that the lòhrens in the east of the land knew even greater longevity magic, but if so they kept that secret to themselves. No matter. Life and death were of no great interest to her after all these years. The one she had had enough of, and the other she no longer feared.

It was time to be moving on. She had a long way to travel, and the more distance she put between herself and whatever had pursued her in the forest, the better.

She dressed. Her clothes were nearly dry again, but as she put them on the sight of her wrinkled body annoyed her. How had she come to this? It was all well and good to believe that a person should be judged by their deeds alone, but she missed the beauty that graced her in her youth.

By the time she strode out of the little wood, those thoughts were gone. She studied the land about as she walked, looking for smoke, which would signal a village or farmstead. She saw nothing. She cast her gaze around, trying to spot the flight of any birds, especially along her backtrail, that might indicate someone was following her. There was no sign of any such thing. She strained her hearing, trying to detect anything out of the ordinary on the plains, but again, all she heard was the whisper of the wind through the grass tops, many going to seed as the warmth of summer faded.

Despite all her checks, she felt increasingly uneasy. That might be expected though. She was in enemy land now, or at least those who had become enemies but might be friends if they had different leaders. Should she be discovered by Nagraks it might be difficult to explain who she was or what she was doing.

That was a problem for later though. She could not remember the last time she had eaten, and hunger gnawed at her stomach. She was dry now, and the fever had been beaten back, but she would need strength soon that only food could give. Ahead was a line of trees that followed a creek or gulley, and it was in such a place as that where she might find tubers, berries or nuts.

She hastened ahead, but slowed when she drew close. Caution guided her, and she had no intention of walking into an area where Nagraks might have gathered.

They might only be herdsmen seeking shelter such as herself while they rested, but anyone who saw her might send word to the shamans if they became suspicious of her.

She saw no sign of anything untoward, and moved as a shadow into the band of trees. It was darker here, and she missed the sunlight. Yet the area was small and she soon discovered that she was alone. More than that, she found food.

It was a little early, yet still there were several hickory trees beginning to drop their nuts. Swiftly she gathered some, and then found two large rocks which she used to shell them. The nut meat tasted good to her, and it was highly nutritious. She ate her fill, and then gathered a supply.

Coming to the edge of the wood, she watched again. Only by caution had she survived so long, and she was not about to give it up now. That sense of unease was on her again, as though she were missing some fact that her illness had washed from her thoughts. Yet there was nothing there to alarm her.

Even so, she waited and kept watching. She had a decision to make too. Where should she go? Her heart yearned to strike out toward Shar and join her. She was not that far away either. Not that it mattered, for the enchantment that connected them enabled her to find Shar wherever she went. Yet now, tantalizingly, she was not far to the east. They could soon be reunited.

But it must not be. Not yet anyway. Everything was for Shar, but she could help her best now by staying away. Shar must grow into being emperor by herself, for only by doing so could she become strong enough to survive by herself in the future that was to come. Moreover, if she and Shar were together they would present a single target to the enemy, which they would dearly love to have. By keeping away from her, she forced the shamans to divide their power. That would cost them, and it was the first rule of war: do what your opposition least wants you to do.

That gave her the next step of the plan that was forming in her mind. What would the enemy least wish? They would hate her in the heart of the Cheng nation, which was Nagrak City. There, she could cause more mischief for them than anywhere else. It was the center of their secular power, as Three Moon Mountain was the center of their magic.

Her mind made up, Shulu left the cover of the little wood and trod with a firm step toward the south. The quicker she reached the city the better, for there she could hide. Out here, by herself as an old woman, some might take her for a shaman, and that would be dangerous for her.

Nagrak City was a place she had not been, at least in the flesh, since Chen Fei had died. The place could only bring back memories that were better left buried. Emotion would drown her if she let it. Even so, her long absence from the place might help her now. While she had not been there for so long a period, that did not mean that she did not have agents there. All the more so because it was one of the few places she chose not to go, so perforce she needed other hands to do her work. The city was full of spies: shaman spying on shaman, chief spying on chief, and among them were her own provocateurs, dormant for generation after generation, yet still ready to do her bidding for the payments they and their ancestors had received. Some, though few, even knew who funded their lifestyle.

She quickened her pace. Once there, she would study the shamans, for nowhere except Three Moon Mountain held so many of them, and she would consider how best to wreak havoc among them.

10. Secrets

Shar chose her words carefully. "The place we go is called The Vale of Nathradin. It's a valley, and a deep one, proving that the flat lands of the Fields of Rah are not quite as flat as many believe."

Asana frowned, and she thought he would be the first to interpret what the name meant. Perhaps he was, but he said nothing. It was Huigar who spoke instead.

"A name of ill omen," she said, clenching her left fist and then opening it palm down as many warriors did as a gesture to ward off evil.

"You know what it means?"

"It means," and she hesitated a moment, "the vale of howling winds," she replied.

Radatan looked uneasy. "Maybe the Smoking Eyes Tribe would render it like that. But Two Ravens folk would interpret it as the vale of screaming spirits."

They were both right. Shulu had told Shar as much herself, but had also said the name was older than the trap that held the shamans. And it had nothing to do with them, nor did it signify anything other than the noise the wind made as it crested stones along the rim of the valley.

"In the Nagrak tongue, where the vale is situated, it just means howling wind. There's no cause for concern in the name, but the danger the shamans might pose is more than real enough."

"How far away is it?" Asana asked.

"A few more days to the west, right into Nagrak territory."

"And you know exactly how to find it?"

"I do. And though deep into Nagrak land, they'll not follow us there if we're found. It's a sacred place to them."

"Are you *sure* the Nagraks mean wind by the name and not spirits? Otherwise, why do they consider it sacred ground?" Huigar asked.

To that, Shar could only shrug. She did not know the answer for sure. Shulu had said one of the reasons she chose the valley as the trap was because there was magic there already.

They talked a little longer on that subject. But Shar could tell them nothing new except there were many large stones cropping up out of the earth at the rim of the valley that the wind curled around or through, and that it sometimes howled. Most of those stones were natural, though some were erected by the hands of men. Yet the Nagraks said their ancestors had not done it.

They rested after that, sleeping in the confines of the hollow while they took shifts during the day to keep watch over the surrounding area. No enemy was seen, and Shar began to think they had escaped the army undetected, as she had hoped.

Dusk settled over the land, and Shar watched a hare as it ventured close to the hollow and then raced away after eventually spotting her where she sat still near the tree.

They were restless to move on, but Shar waited until night fell. She did not trust this land. There were enemies within it, and eyes that might be watching from a hidden place just as they themselves had watched throughout the day.

When they finally strode out of the hollow though, she led them swiftly, and she did not travel in the exact same direction she had been going the day before. If they were being somehow watched, this would make it harder to predict their final destination.

Thus they traveled for a few days, and the peace of the land was alluring, yet still Shar mistrusted it.

Another dawn came, swiftly casting light over the grasslands like a bowl of bright water overturned on a table, and Shar found shelter in an old grove of trees. It could not be called a wood, for it was scarcely more than a few old trees that had somehow sprung to life in isolation amid all the grass, and now, in age, with rotting trunks and falling branches, seemed destined soon to be swallowed by the earth and turned to grass again.

Beneath the cover of the leaves they settled down and established a camp. There were signs that cattle frequented the place, for the ground was heavily trod and their hoofmarks showed in the dust. Likewise, the lower branches were all trimmed at an even height, the same which a beast might reach by stretching up its neck.

"There must be water close by," Radatan observed. "At least within several miles."

Shar thought that was likely true, for the beasts must drink. Yet they might merely drink from a wallow scarcely fit for a person to use. Still, they had to find somewhere to replenish their waterbags soon.

They settled down, and after a brief meal Huigar took the first watch while the others prepared to sleep. The young woman moved out to the perimeter of the trees where she could obtain a view, but returned soon afterward before anyone had fallen asleep.

"There are strange birds in the sky," she said. "They're not eagles, but they fly in a similar manner."

Shar was alert straight away. It might be that they were discovered, and the shamans might use other birds than eagles to spy out the land.

They all went to the rim of the trees, and carefully peered out.

"I've not seen their like before," Huigar said.

"Nor I," Radatan agreed.

Shar glanced at the birds from beneath the concealment of a branch. Instantly, she knew what they were. Such birds were seen in Tsarin Fen, but evidently did not like the Wahlum Hills where both Huigar and Radatan came from, and who had traveled little or not at all away from their clan.

"They're called ibis," Shar told them.

"The Nagraks," Asana added, "call them *nagga-snagga* birds."

Shar laughed at that. At least in Tsarin Fen that would be translated as smelly-greedy, which was an apt name for them.

"Might they be the eyes of the shamans," Huigar asked, "just as eagles can be?"

It was a good question, and Shar wished she knew the answer. There was a flock of them, and they circled high on rising currents of air. They had the perfect vantage to spy out movement across the grasslands, but whether or not an ibis could see with the acuity of an eagle, she did not know. There were so many things she wished she had asked Shulu while she had the chance, but she could not now. Suddenly, she missed her, but forced her mind back to the matter at hand.

"You did well to bring our attention to them," she told Huigar. "They might or might not serve as the eyes of the shamans, but we must assume they can. We'll keep traveling by night."

The rest of them went back to their camp then, leaving Huigar to continue the first watch. Shar had hoped to slip away from the army undetected. If they had somehow been discovered, then the danger to them was immense. She would not feel safe until she reached the Vale of Nathradin, for that was a barrier to shamans and Nagraks alike. Only Shar could get through the enchantment, but in doing so she would exchange one danger for another.

Shar drifted to sleep, but all she could see with her inner vision were the ibis, circling in a group, gaining height and soaring with grace in the skies. It was a thing she had seen a thousand times in the fens, but now it worried her.

Perhaps because of the ibis, she dreamed of growing up in the fens, and that meant dreaming of her grandmother too. She walked the dim paths of the swamp with her, and a storm built in the south, clouds towering upon clouds, lightning flashing from the dark, seething mass.

A storm comes, Shulu announced, pointing at it with her long, bony arm. *It will be such a storm as the land has never seen before. Yet after the rains, the grass will grow greener than you have ever seen.*

She was woken by Radatan late in the day to take the last watch, but the sense of Shulu stayed with her. It felt as though she were close despite it being just a dream. The ibis were gone. The sky was clear, nor could anything be seen moving across the open expanse of the plains. Even so, the worry that had nagged her sleep did not lessen.

Dusk was approaching when she woke the others and they shared another meal. As much as Shar loved being in the wild, she would have enjoyed it more if only they could have lit a fire and eaten something warm. Yet the cautious side of her nature forbade that, and it preferred safety to comfort.

"Are the nagga-snagga birds gone?" Asana asked. He had taken the second watch of the day and the birds had still been visible then.

"Gone," Shar told him simply. Whether they had just flown out of sight or continued on their migration, for Shulu had told her the birds winged southward even over the Eagle Claw Mountains in search of warmer climes this time of year, she did not know. It was time to put them from her mind though. She could not allow herself to fear every shadow she saw.

The sun dropped low, and they were ready to depart but still waiting for darkness to come. Asana drew his sword and began to play a routine with it as he often did. Shar understood. A perfectionist such as he must practice every day, otherwise their skill did not grow. She herself often did the same thing.

The swordmaster began slowly. Each move was fluid and graceful, yet precise. Then he gathered speed. His feet skipped lightly over the ground like a mountain goat leaping, sure-of-foot, from rocky ledge to crag. Even as his weight shifted from foot to foot, the sword drew back in perfectly timed deflections or thrusts. He was one with the sword, the slightest movement of his body adding power to its tip, and the deft movement of his waist, in unison with the blade, timed to deflect an attack with the minimum of exertion.

Then he moved faster, the sword a blur of speed in the gathering gloom, yet still his body shifted with that same effortless grace. In a lesser swordsman, that greater speed would cause slight imperfections in technique, yet not so with Asana. He deserved the title of gan, and more beside. He was a master such as she had never seen, and despite that she had watched him practice many times before she was still spellbound. His skill was breathtaking, and she knew, despite all her training, she would not be a match for him. The thought rankled her momentarily, but then she used it as she always did to spur herself to greater efforts. He was older than she. If she persisted, one day she might reach his level of accomplishment.

Asana finished, and when he sheathed his sword and stood still a few moments, she noticed he was barely breathing hard. She wished she knew his secret for that, but then she felt guilty. He had told her often enough that there was no secret, and it would come to her with practice. But she held a secret from him, and the others. She still had not quite told them all that she knew of the Vale of Nathradin.

11. We Have Been Found

The companions traveled for several nights, fleeting shadows across the night-darkened plains. They shunned the daylight, slept while others in the world worked, and became used to seeing by starlight alone.

There was a comradeship among them. Despite all being from different tribes, and having different backgrounds, they toiled together as one. They were, and always would be, their own individual selves. Yet they worked in harmony for a common goal. In them, Shar saw not just her friends but the future of the Cheng nation. What individuals could do, so too could entire tribes.

Becoming an empire did not mean enforcing a single culture and set of beliefs on all, decided upon by some elite class of rulers who were somehow wiser than everyone else. It meant rejoicing in all their differences, yet coming together, when they chose to, for the common good.

Shar was brooding one night on these thoughts, as she often did, and wondering if she could ever turn such dreams into reality, when she heard a wolf howl in the distance. She paid it no heed, for wolves were common enough.

The howl was taken up by others though soon after, and it seemed to come from along their backtrail.

"I don't like it," Radatan said.

Huigar said nothing, but her hand drifted down to her sword hilt as she walked. Asana seemed unperturbed, but he always did. He would face an army rushing at him with the same calm expression he would give to a merchant peddling his wares.

Shar followed his example, but when next they heard the howling it was still on the backtrail, but closer.

"We have been found," Shar said.

"Wolves don't hunt people," Asana said, but there was doubt in his voice. He guessed what she knew.

"Wolves might not, but the shamans can make them. Or maybe they just sound like wolves. Shamans can summon creatures from other worlds. Or even make them."

They moved ahead rapidly. "How could we have been found?" Radatan asked.

"A spy in the camp, probably," Shar said. "News of my leaving the army might have been withheld for a little while, but eventually it would have got out. And then we may have been seen from the air. Maybe the ibis, although we avoided them well. But there are birds that fly at night, too."

Shar made a decision. She and Radatan were the best at finding a trail, or hiding it. Only she had magic in her swords though.

"Take the lead, Radatan. Travel swiftly, and try to find paths that leave as little trail as possible. Where the wolves go, it might be that humans ride with them. I'll guard the rear."

Huigar seemed about to object, for she lived and breathed for her role as bodyguard, but she picked her battles. She would not win this one, and she knew it. Shar had the magic swords, and her skill as a scout meant she also had the best chance of detecting any enemy coming up close behind them. That was an advantage that might save all their lives.

The wolves were silent now, perhaps just following the scent of their prey. Or maybe they had lost it. Shar did not think so though.

Radatan employed all the skills of the hunter. He took them by changing paths, at whiles over grass, but where possible through trees and along gulleys. Some even held water, and here they walked hastily through it for hundreds of feet at a time before veering to the side. Once, on doing so, they were lucky enough to find a stand of willows which they climbed and moved from branch to branch to try to hide their scent.

Shar had little faith in any of it. Not because of any lack in Radatan's skill, but rather because it was not easy to fool the senses of a beast, and even water would not be enough unless wide and deep.

Even so, there had been no sound of any pursuit for an hour or two. Afar in the east there were signs the dawn was coming. The stars glittered coldly from the dark sky, but they were not quite so bright. The grass was thick with dew and their air had become perfectly still. It was like the world had taken a deep breath in preparation for the bustle of the coming day.

They trod on, weary shadows wending across the grass, and when the sky began to lighten even Shar felt that maybe they had been too quick to fear pursuit, and that they had overreacted.

Yet that growing light seemed to act as a signal, for all at once the howling began again. It came from their backtrail, only it was much closer this time, and the animals were spread out in a semicircle.

"The net closes," Asana warned.

No one answered. They pushed on harder, and daylight found them jogging across the Fields of Rah. They looked back at times, but saw nothing. Yet they would not. Not yet, anyway. Wolves were small, the grass was often deep, and they remained some way behind them.

"I think your tricks worked, Radatan," Shar said.

"How do you figure that?" the hunter asked.

"Because without them we would have been surrounded before now. In the dark. Now, the daylight gives us a better chance to fight."

He grunted at that. "Maybe, but I'm not ready to give up just yet. If we keep going, we may reach a village or farmstead where we can barricade the doors and windows. I'd rather not fight a pack of wolves."

They raced ahead, traveling as fast as they could while not exhausting themselves. They had to keep fresh enough to fight if it came to that, and Shar knew it would. A village of Nagraks might not help them, even if they did not know who they were. And she sensed the shamans behind this, either controlling the wolves or that they were not wolves but some kind of summoning. Either way, the wolves would not give up, and the fragile timber of a hut would not stand forever against tooth and claw if driven by sorcery.

They ran through the morning. The howling came at intervals, but aways it drew closer rather than farther away. Shar wondered if the wolves were toying with them. It was possible. They should have caught up by now.

"Radatan!" she called. "Look for a good defensive position. These wolves are trying to run us into the ground. They're trying to tire us. Only when we're exhausted will they attack. Better to stand and fight now than let that happen."

She did not think they would find a good place. Yet not long after she gave that order Radatan led them up a slight slope. It was rocky ground, and the grass was short. At the top was a tumbled ruin of boulders. They were not large, but they were large enough to offer some protection. Shar leaped to the top of one, and from her high vantage she looked around. There was nothing else to see in any direction that would be a better place to fight.

"We'll make our stand here," she declared.

12. The Eyes of the Enemy

Kubodin took command of the army, but his heart was with Shar. Yet if he were to serve her properly, he must do his best to put her from his mind and sharpen his every thought toward one purpose: gaining Chatchek fortress and fortifying its decaying defenses against the enemy.

It was time to put aside his act as well. Most took him for a wild hill man, fond of drinking, gambling and fighting. Even wild hill men took him for that. Asana and Shar did not. He was a chieftain now, and born of a long line of them. He had learned military tactics since he was three years old. He spoke more languages than most of the learned men of the land, and read widely of poetry, philosophy and science. He was the opposite of all he appeared to be, and hiding it caused his enemies to underestimate him.

That would not work now on the shamans. They would destroy the army if they could, and it did not matter who led it. Likewise, those he led must see that he was competent. Otherwise they would not follow, and that would start first with the other chiefs despite their promises to Shar.

Several days passed without incident. With Radatan gone, he ensured the scouts reported directly to him. The greatest asset in a military campaign was not the larger army, but the better information. He ensured the flow of that information came to him. So far, there were no reports of the enemy. That would not last though. Every time he saw a scout approach, he expected to hear word that they had been seen.

It was luck that they had not been, for the most part. Some was attributable to Shar. She had sent more mixed signals to them than a teenage girl did to a bevy of admirers.

He could not rest on her achievements though. He must continue in a like vein, so one evening he called the chiefs to him.

"Gentlemen," he began, "the enemy is watching us. We know their scouts are here, for we've captured some. Likewise, the shamans are sure to be watching from the skies. What they don't know yet, and what we must keep from them, are our intentions."

Dakashul narrowed his eyes. "What's this? I see you speak, and I hear your words. You're Kubodin but not Kubodin."

He shrugged. "I'm still Kubodin. But there's a side to me that few have seen save my friends, and even them but rarely. That's the Kubodin needed now."

"What's your plan to further confuse the enemy?" Nahring asked. "I guess that you have one."

"I do. A simple one. It comes with a little danger though. I would rather not split our army, but my plan calls for that. If for no other reason than it's the last thing we should be doing right now, and therefore the action that will confound the enemy the most. They won't understand why we're doing it, and they'll waste a lot of time trying to figure it out."

Argash leaned forward, and a smile was on his lips. "I like it. It seems just the sort of thing Shar would do. So what's the exact plan?"

It was a compliment to be compared to Shar, and Kubodin knew it. He was older and more experienced, but she had an instinct for tactics that no amount of learning could match.

"It's simple enough. Tomorrow I'll lead one half of the army, and Nahring will lead the other half. I'll veer a little westward, and Nahring will veer a little to the east. Then we'll converge in two days' time. The enemy will wonder if we've had a disagreement, or if we just have different objectives. That will confuse them, but most of all … it'll keep their attention on us and help keep their eyes away from Shar."

Argash seemed pleased. Nahring looked thoughtful, however.

"What is it?" Kubodin asked.

The Smoking Eyes chief sighed. "It's a good idea. It just worries me that if my command is attacked by sorcery, we have no defense."

"Ah, yes. That's true," Kubodin agreed. "But that's why I'm taking the westward route, closer to the enemy. You should be at less risk. Still, Shar was right. We're all vulnerable against magic, and her swords and my axe were never going to be enough. We *need* those shamans she seeks."

The next morning the plan was put into action, and the army divided and began to march. Kubodin was anxious about it though. He would not be easy until the two forces rejoined. Things could go wrong, and he did not like giving command of so many warriors to someone ese. Yet Nahring had proved himself, and he was loyal to Shar.

He trudged forward at the head of the army, and he pulled his hood up for the first part of the morning. It was growing cold of late, and the wind on these plains had nothing to stop it. Even a breeze cut through his clothes, and he shivered for a while until walking warmed him up.

The Fields of Rah seemed a strange place to him. Unlike most Cheng, he had traveled widely. Even outside the lands of the Cheng, which were vast enough, he had wandered far with Asana. But always he preferred a land of hills and forests like his home. When this was over, if he survived it all, it was time to settle down in the Wahlum Hills and raise a family.

He walked with Argash. The two of them had become friends. Perhaps that was because of all the chiefs, they were the two who were closest to Shar.

"Was she always like she is now?" he asked.

Argash knew exactly who he meant. He grinned, and looked suddenly much younger.

"I knew her even as a child. She was stubborn then, and she's stubborn now. You don't get anywhere in life without that trait, though some prefer to call it determination. She really hasn't changed. She's just grown up, got more skilled and become more confident. All that's different is the color of her eyes. I struggle to get used to that violet gaze." Argash paused in thought. "How did that come about? I've often wondered but never thought to ask."

Kubodin waved a fly away from his face. "You're not the only one who finds her gaze … challenging. I've seen it strike fear into her enemies and devotion into her followers."

"How did they change color though?"

"I was there," Kubodin replied. "It was an eerie thing to see. The way I understand it, Shulu Gan used magic to disguise them, and the spell was broken when Shar won the Swords of Dawn and Dusk." He clicked his fingers together. "Just like that they changed color, and though I believed she was the descendant of the emperor before then, in that moment I *knew*, and a chill ran through me. It was a moment of magic."

Argash said nothing for a little while. "And is it true that the woman I knew as Go Shan is really Shulu Gan?"

"So Shar told me, but I never met her in that guise. I did meet Shulu when this began though, Taga Nashu, the grandmother who does not die, as legend calls her, and she is one that inspires trust and fear at the same time. I'm glad to be on her side, and I wouldn't want her as an enemy for all the world."

Argash seemed to shudder, and then he shook his head and half smiled.

"To think, as a youth, that I once threw eggs at the walls of her hut…"

Kubodin burst out in laughter. "What did she do?"

"What any grandmother would do to a naughty child. She scolded me, and glared at me with eyes that fair sent a shiver up my spine."

Kubodin kept laughing, and Argash bit his lip. "It's not that funny. Think of what she could have done to me had she wished."

With an effort, Kubodin stopped laughing. "It's good to know that she didn't do anything though. Had you done that to the village shaman, I suspect you would have got worse treatment."

"Indeed," Argash said. "Another boy I knew once ate plums from the tree at the back of the shaman's hut. He was whipped for that. So Shulu was good to me by comparison. The next day she even gave me some fresh-baked honey biscuits. But I never forgot the glare of her eyes from the day before."

The army made good time, and each hour that passed without the scouts bringing news of the enemy was a relief to Kubodin. That afternoon though, they slowed. The weather was turning against them. A cold wind blew hard from the north, and this bit through them. With it came an overcast sky, and at times it drizzled. It was a sign of the winter to come, yet no doubt there were still many more warm and sunny days of the year left.

Perhaps the shamans thought no army would strike at Nagrak City at this time of year. Maybe that was why they had sent no force out to harass them. Or maybe they were building a force out of reach of his scouts, for they could only penetrate so far into enemy territory.

The night was cold and wet, but by dawn the sky was bright and the wind had stilled to the faintest movement of air. All through their marching Kubodin and Nahring had kept in touch by riders, and nothing untoward had occurred. Yet Nahring had been slowed because he veered around a significant sized forest. His scouts reported it was empty, but caution dictated he did not try to lead his army through it.

"He'll meet you for the noontide rest," the latest rider told him. Kubodin dismissed him with a simple "good work" and it only occurred to him as the man led his pony away that he did not know, nor could even guess, what tribe the rider hailed from. Shar had done an incredible job of breaking down the clan barriers that had divided the nation for a thousand years. Who knew what she could do if she actually became emperor?

Not long after he heard the first bad news of his command. It was a young man who gave it to him, barely twenty years old, if that. Yet his eyes were sharp and he spoke with confidence.

"Nagrak riders have been spotted, sir. Some fifty of them twenty miles away."

Kubodin thought quickly. That was more riders than most single villages could muster, but it was hardly a large force.

"Were they discovered, or did they allow themselves to be seen?"

The man, youth though he was, understood the distinction.

"So far as we can tell, they were surprised to see us and hastened away when they did."

"Good. If they had allowed themselves to be seen, more likely than not it was some sort of distraction intended to make us focus on them while their true force drew closer to us from another direction. So probably there's an army behind them. Were more scouts sent to check that out?"

"Yes, sir."

"Good lad. Have a drink of water and rest for a moment. You've earned it."

Kubodin called the chiefs to him and told them the news. There was nothing to be done at this stage though save to press ahead. This they did, but the army was now at a higher sense of alert. He ensured word of the riders spread so that it would be no surprise if soon they heard of an opposing army. Their days of easy, if swift, marching were over. Battle loomed, and if anything was so surprising it was how far they had been able to come before that prospect eventuated.

They camped at noon, and the sun was warm. Whatever moisture was on the grass and in the top layer of earth from the night before had dried out. Of Nahring, there was no sign. Yet word came from a rider that they were close, and soon after the second half of Shar's army came into view.

Kubodin breathed a sigh of relief. Maybe the maneuver had served no purpose. Or maybe it had held off an enemy attack while they tried to decide what was happening. Either way, it felt good to be one whole army again, and he shook Nahring's hand warmly.

After a rest, longer than usual, they marched again. Kubodin was cautious though, and he chose to halt the army half an hour early. It was later in the afternoon, but dusk had not yet started. However, they came to a favorable defensive position, being higher ground bordered by a swift running creek on one side, and gave orders to establish a camp. If the enemy pressed ahead toward him overnight, they would not catch him unprepared or on unfavorable terrain.

As the sun set and the long shadows of evening marched over the land, several riders came in. They were scouts, and they approached Kubodin with haste. They leaped off their mounts and saluted him.

"What news, lads?" he asked.

The oldest of them spoke, but he, like most of the scouts, was still quite young.

"We've seen several groups of riders, on and off. But before they tried to attack us, we saw beyond them. An army is gathered to the northwest, but it's small."

"How small?"

"We could only see a thousand men, all of them mounted. There could be more, but if so they were farther away and out of view."

Kubodin was not surprised. "Good work. Get some rest now."

The riders jumped back on their mounts and trotted away, leaving Kubodin by himself and thoughtful.

The enemy force was not strong. Still, they were mounted and that gave them speed to strike and retreat. They could try to harass him, or even launch a night attack. He would be prepared for that, and to that end he ordered the sentries to be doubled and the scouts to be on the alert, and to spread a wide net around Shar's army.

It was possible this was just an advanced force of Nagraks, serving as the eyes of the enemy, and others were on the way. They could be of different tribes, probably on foot, or more Nagraks. Certainly this was just a fraction of the riders the Nagraks could muster.

It worried him though that the force they knew about was nearly, if not quite, blocking the path he intended to take to Chatchek Fortress. Could it be that they had somehow guessed, or learned, of Shar's plan for the army and its destination? Might they try to prevent him from reaching it?

All things were possible, and he sent messages for the chiefs to join him. They had much to discuss.

13. The Vision of the Blades

Shar remained poised atop the boulder. If it were her fate to die here, torn to shreds by wolves, then she would meet her end square on.

The others climbed to the top of boulders also. It was some advantage against the beasts, but they were not so high as to be able to clamber out of reach.

The plain seemed empty, then suddenly Shar saw movement in the grass. Then there was more a little to the left. A moment later she spotted the wolves themselves. They were much closer than she had thought, and they had truly been trying to tire their quarry before attacking, even as she had surmised earlier.

At a howl from one of them, more appeared. They had been slinking through the grass on their bellies, but now they trotted forward in the open and there were several groups of three or four each.

"They don't hunt like wolves," Radatan said.

Huigar answered him. "They *look* like wolves though, and nothing more."

It seemed to Shar that the tone of her friend's voice posed a question, even if the words themselves did not.

"They're wolves," Shar replied. "But prepare yourself for more than that. One way or another, they're under the influence of shamans. They're no longer dumb beasts, but guided by intelligence."

It was not long before the wolves came close. They circled the boulders some thirty or forty feet away, lips peeled back and growling. The sound was hideous, and Shar felt fear run through her body. Yet when the animals drew a little closer, the great cold that always overcame her during periods of extreme danger settled over her, and fear was replaced with determination.

"We'll give them a fight to remember," she said, her voice cold as ice as she drew the Swords of Dawn and Dusk.

A thrill ran through her when she drew the blades. Their magic was alive. She did not approve of what Shulu had done to forge such weapons, and yet she would be dead long ago without them. The niceties of the philosophers were often challenged by cruel reality, and found wanting.

The wolves gathered closer, snarling and gnashing their teeth. It seemed to her that fear was on them, but a compulsion guided them over and above that, one that could not be set aside. It was the work of the shamans.

Radatan threw a rock at one, but missed. The beast backed away a few steps, but then came closer, its pack mates with it.

They were close now. They ringed the boulders, and Shar could see their eyes. It seemed to her that there was nothing unusual about the creatures. They were natural animals rather than summonings or creations of dark sorcery. And yet, there was a kind of shimmering about them.

She turned around, glancing at those behind her. Huigar was there, facing the other way. They were not quite back-to-back, but they each offered protection for the other.

When she spun around to the front again, several of the wolves there had rushed in closer while her back was turned. They could almost try to jump up to the boulders now themselves. She gripped the Swords of Dawn and Dusk harder.

Even as she did so the strange shimmer she had seen intensified and then suddenly became clearer. She looked with her own eyes, yet she saw with the magic of the swords too.

The wolves were merely wolves, and she saw the spark of life within them, coursing through their arteries, penetrating every particle of their flesh and radiating outward from their bodies in an aura that pulsed and surged. Yet within that brightness was a shadow, hunched down, compressed, conforming to the shape of the wolf yet not of the wolf at all.

It was hard to see, yet those shadowy images were the spirits of the shamans. Their magic flowed over the long miles from wherever their bodies were, perhaps even as far away as Three Moon Mountain, and brought the essence of themselves here to control the wolves.

Shar's eyes darted from one wolf to another. All were the same. Within each crouched such a figure, shadowy, vague, but certainly human. She saw they were all old men, long haired and ancient. Some were not just shamans, but likely shaman elders, and her hatred of the enemy that had killed her forefather, enslaved the land and would kill her flared to life.

She did not hesitate. Some wild emotion took her mind, wresting it from that calm tranquility that had descended just moments ago. She did not resist, but followed its urging, knowing in some rational corner of her mind that looked down on all this as though from afar that surprise was always the best attack.

Yelling a battle cry she leaped down off the boulder into the very midst of the wolves, her eyes flashing and The Swords of Dawn and Dusk spinning arcs of death.

Even as she landed the wolves scattered, but two died that were not quick enough. One was slashed through its throat, red blood gushing into the thick fur. Another had its guts spilled onto the grass.

Shar saw the spirit forms of the shamans writhe as though in pain, then like flashing shadows they arced away from the bodies they had possessed. Whether they would die as did the wolves, she was not sure. She hoped so, but feared not.

She spun around at some noise behind her, the Sword of Dawn glittering as it hewed off the head of a wolf that darted at her leg to hamstring her. Another wolf growled close by, and she leaped toward it causing it to jump back in turn. Then there were more battle cries, and her companions were down with her on the ground, weapons flaying around and blood flowing.

It was too much for the wolves. Their natural fear overcame the will of the shamans who dominated them, and they scattered and fled. Yet not far. They stopped and gathered some fifty feet away, and Shar could see the shamans within straining to make them attack again.

"Hear me, shamans!" she cried out. "Come and face me in person, if you dare! Come! I'm here, you cowards who murder children. Are you men or are you lower than the maggots that feast on carcasses? Come! I see you hunkering there inside the wolves. I see you, and I hate you! I will kill you all!"

The wolves howled, and some bit themselves as though they sensed something wrong within them that they must try to remove. Some slinked away overcoming the shamans inside them. But most bared their fangs and growled, beginning to edge closer.

Shar turned to her companions. "To the boulders again."

They leaped up, taking the high ground once more. The wolves raced in, but her daring before to jump among them had paid a profit. Quite a few were dead, and some had disappeared from sight. Those who were left were only a handful, and their chances of killing their quarry was reduced.

Yet still the wolves came on with terrible wrath. The shamans who controlled them had broken the will of the beasts again, and drove them with a fury more primitive than any that nature bestowed upon all its multitude of creatures. Only men hated, and that animosity gleamed wickedly in the eyes of the wolves before Shar now, even if the emotion that flashed from them was not their own.

She gripped tight the swords. The hunkered form of the shamans within the beasts became clearer. She had known that the magic in the blades had worked for Chen Fei, and that it would work for her. Yet Shulu had warned her that the magic was alive, and it would respond to different wielders in different fashions according to their character. She had still to learn all the uses she could put the blades to.

Even so, their primary magic was still in their sharp edge, just as any sword, and she used that now. A wolf leaped up at her, its paws scrabbling over the rock surface as it simultaneously tried to tear the flesh of her legs and gain solid footing atop the boulder with her.

The Sword of Dusk came down, driven with all Shar's strength, and with that the lowering of her weight. The tip pierced flesh and bone, severing the spine and penetrating deep into the creature. Hot blood spilled forth, yet she sensed something else as well.

The tip of the blade struck also the shadowy form of the shaman, and he squirmed inside trying to flee. Almost he was away, ready to flit from the beast and escape. The magic in the blade seemed to cause him great pain, and she turned and twisted it inside the beast now seeking not to kill just it but the shaman also.

Driving her weight lower, but now at a new angle, she felt a flash of power at its tip. The wolf screamed, but it was the voice of a man in agony. Suddenly both beast and shadow were still. The animal was dead, and so too the shaman. The shadow did not leave the body, but it disintegrated, and through the magic in the blades she sensed the last breath of the shaman far away.

She kicked the corpse of the wolf off the boulder, and looked around to see a similar fight was occurring with her friends. Asana had killed two wolves already, and Radatan and Huigar were fending off theirs. Even as she looked, another leapt at her, and she struck at it.

So the fight continued. It did not last long though. Shar killed several wolves, and so too the shamans within them. She did not think the others were doing this, but certainly they killed their wolves, and after a little while, those left alive, turned and fled.

Even as they did so, one that Shar had not seen leapt at her from the side. Too late she turned to defend herself, and it smashed into her knocking her off the boulder and onto the ground. The beast was atop her, searching for her neck with its slavering jaws.

Then Huigar was there on the ground beside her. She dared not use her sword lest she hit Shar, but her knife plunged into the body of the creature. Blood gushed from its mouth over Shar, but it still tried to tear her throat away. Yet it was weaker, and she threw it off. As she did so, Radatan killed it.

Shar rose quickly to her feet, swords in hand. She looked around, but of the wolves all she could see were a few here and there rushing away. Yet many dead ones lay about.

"Thank you!" she said to Huigar and Radatan. "It nearly had me."

"It was the last of them," Asana said. He stood upon the farthest boulder, and he was casting his gaze around in all directions. "If we're going to go anywhere, now is the time before they regroup."

He was right. The shamans had been defeated, but not beaten. Soon, they would regain control over the wolves. Or find more. Or do something else. Whatever they may try, the only safe place was now the vale.

"Hurry, then," Shar said. "We have to reach the Vale of Nathradin. They cannot follow us there."

They looked at her doubtfully. "What is this magic barrier," Asana asked, voicing all their concerns, "that can keep shamans locked within, and shamans locked without, that you may yet pass through?"

She had not told them all, but there was no time now.

"Trust me," she replied.

No one argued, and they followed swiftly as she led them away. Even so, she had read on Asana's face that he was beginning to understand. Of them all, he was the most learned in magic, even if he possessed none himself. She was not quite sure of that though. Rumor suggested that he had the power of foresight, and there was *something* about his sword.

It was a beautiful day, and the sun shone warmly from a clear sky with scarcely a breeze to rustle among the seedheads of the dying grasses. Yet it was cold to Shar, and fear closed in on her.

The shamans were coming for her. They would waste no time, nor spare any effort. She was vulnerable away from the army, and they would take advantage of that. Kill her, and they killed the rebellion. Yet she dreaded meeting those shamans who had once served her forefather. They had betrayed him, and they might kill her, or give her up to the enemy. Fear drove her footsteps faster, dread slowed them down. She struggled in silence as she led her friends forward, yet her choices had been made back at the camp, and there was nothing to do now but put her plan into action, if she could.

14. The Warning of the Skulls

The companions raced over the grassland. Shar led them now, for she knew what landmarks to look for that signified the vale was close.

Of the wolves, there was no sign. They had been soundly beaten, but Shar knew in her heart it would not be for long. The shamans had nearly killed her, and that would embolden them to try even harder.

"Look to the sky!" Asana called from behind.

Shar did so. It was the ibis again, and they drifted in slow circles, yet they did so straight above. All her plans were thrown out. She could not hide through the day, nor had they slept as they should have done. On top of that, she set a grueling pace, dividing their journey into spells of swift marching and actual jogging. All these things combined were bad enough, but the longer it went on the worse it became. They would be exhausted if they must fight again, and that would be the end of them.

She gritted her teeth, and pressed ahead. "Ignore them," she called back. "The shamans already know where we are, but I don't think they guess yet where we go. And we're getting close now."

She was not certain of that last point. She had never been here, but Shulu had described the landscape to her in detail from all approaches. Coming from the direction she did, she saw the signs that she had been looking for. The little rise where they had fought off the wolves was the first of them. The grasslands dried out around here, Shulu had said. The soil was thinner and rockier, and the slope of the land not quite flat anymore but angling uphill, if by a small degree.

"See there!" Shar called to the others, and she pointed. In the distance a village could be seen. No smoke rose from it, meaning that it likely was abandoned. "That is Nagralak Village, I believe. We're on course to the vale, and I know exactly where we are."

"It looks abandoned," Huigar said. "Maybe we should go there for shelter?"

"Maybe," Shar replied. "But what then? The shamans would come for us again, and though the wolves might not get into a village hut, at least a well-built one, how long before the shamans send warriors?"

Huigar did not answer. There was no need. They all knew the shamans would not give up, and that the wolves, and worse, would be after them again shortly.

Shar skirted around the village, being sure not to be visible. Magrig had said the land was deserted, and it probably was. The inhabitants had fled fearing an invasion, and would have fallen back to some defensible place where an army would build. Yet she could not be certain of that. There might be enemies within, perhaps even now being roused by a shaman. Despite that it delayed her reaching the vale, she took the long way around.

It might have been an error. She could not know, but in the distance she heard the first howl of a wolf again.

"Hurry," she said, and led the others into a jog once more.

They needed no urging. Few sounds in the wild were as mysterious and human as the howl of a wolf, and few more inspiring of fear if they hunted.

The afternoon was upon them now. Weariness weighed them down. They were tired from running, fighting, and most of all from lack of sleep.

"We're close to safety now," Shar urged them on. "Have faith."

She was not sure if she were reassuring them, or herself.

They raced onward, and even Shar who was used to running all day in Tsarin Fen, felt her legs begin to ache and tire. They could not go on like this for much longer.

Yet the countryside gave her hope. It was changing quickly. There were many small woods, though none provided any protection or chance to lose a pursuit. The ground kept rising at a slight incline, and the rocky nature of the soil became more pronounced. The valley she sought was close now, desperately close, and it was only a question of how near the wolves were and if they would overtake their quarry sooner rather than later.

That question was answered by a terrible howl only a mile or so away. Others took up the call a little farther behind. There was a frenzy to the sound now. The shamans were sparing no effort to push the beasts into this hunt, and she wondered if somehow more shaman elders, of greater power, now possessed the wolves.

They crested a small hill, and there Shar called a halt. They must rest, if only for a few moments, and it was a good place to observe their backtrail.

At once they saw several groups of wolves loping toward them. They were mere dots on the faraway grasslands, but the distance would be made up in a handful of minutes. Time was running out.

There were not only wolves though. "See there," Asana said, pointing to the left. "Those are dogs."

Shar looked and saw. Faintly, over the distance, she heard the barking of them, and she knew at once that the shamans controlled them too. Some were large, some smaller. They did not run at the same speed, and some would be more dangerous than others. Yet between them and the wolves, she, and her friends, would be eaten alive if they did not reach the valley soon.

"Run!" she cried, and led them off again even faster than before, but she did not panic and run at full pace yet.

The afternoon was growing old. On the higher ground ahead of them, pockets of fog began to form. The air was cooling quickly, and night was not that far off.

Shar led them into a patch of fog. It would not hide their scent, but it would, perhaps, make the creatures that followed them a little wary and slow them down.

They entered a rocky gulley and scrambled up its winding course. Shar fell, hurting her knee, but rose swiftly and raced ahead. She kept a closer eye on her footing. The last thing she needed now was an injury that prevented her from running.

"By Aranloth's age!" cried Radatan. "What on earth is that?"

Shar saw what he meant. At the head of the gulley that they were just now exiting, a pole had been sunk into the ground. At its top was fixed a sheep's skull.

"It's a warning to stay away from this area," Shar called back. "It means we're close. Hurry!"

Haste was needed. The wolves were howling nearby now, and the frenzied yapping of the dogs was closing in. The gulley had slowed Shar down, but it would not slow the four-footed pursuers as much.

The grasslands were gone now. All about them was a sea of fog, and Shar could see nothing of their backtrail. She pushed ahead, finding a winding way uphill. The slope had increased and the path was difficult. Not just because it was a steeper climb, but because the ground was very rocky.

There was another pole with a skull on it, this one seemingly ancient. The timber was half rotted by age, and it was no longer straight but leaning like a man who staggered. The skull was cracked and weathered by time, sitting lopsided at the top. The effect was more frightening than the previous one. Almost it seemed like some skeletal old man warning them away from a place of death.

Shar ignored it. Death was behind them, and gaining fast. Right now, she would jump into any danger because it could hardly be worse than what she already faced.

The fog swirled thick about them. It was hard to see, and it muted the sound of the pursuit. It was close though, and even as she raced ahead she thought she saw sleek forms flit in and out of sight at the edges of her field of vision.

She drew her swords, thinking to be ready in case of attack. None came, yet the swords glimmered with an eldritch light. It was, she surmised, some reaction to magic. The fog was not natural, but rather a part of the great spell Shulu had cast long ago.

She looked behind her. All her companions had drawn their weapons also, and their faces glimmered paly in the light of her swords.

"We're nearly there," she whispered. She dared not call out loudly lest she give away their exact position to some beast that lay in wait nearby.

More skull-topped poles loomed in and out of the fog. She slowed to a walk. Howls, growls and barks multiplied in the fog all around them, but she found what she was looking for. They had reached the top of the slope they had been climbing. She could not see ahead nor behind, but she could tell because the ground, as she had expected, leveled out.

There was a path marked by rocks to either side, and this she followed. There were no more warnings. Those who erected them dared not come this close to the valley.

At last she saw, rising up out of the fog and strangely catching the light of her swords, two massive pillars of stone. It was one of the entrances to the Vale of Nathradin, and it stood before her like a gateway to another world. Which, in truth, she knew it was.

Yet even as excitement gripped her that she had found the place she needed, and strode toward it, Asana called out from behind.

"We must stand and fight!"

Shar spun around and saw what he had. Wolves and dogs were loping out of the fog behind them, only paces away.

15. Committed to Battle

The smoke swirled thickly from the fire, due to a branch with leaves still upon it having been placed there. Kubodin loved the smell of it, but he did not believe, as some of the other chiefs did, that it was the breath of the gods. Still less that it brought wise counsels.

Wise counsels were needed though.

"An army approaches us," he told the chiefs. "It stands between us and Chatchek fortress, or close enough to that to make me wonder if they guess our destination and try to block us."

"How large?" Argash asked.

"A token force only. There are a thousand riders, almost certainly Nagraks."

"It's nothing," Dakashul said. "Let's go straight at them, and crush them. They'll flee before ever a sword is drawn though."

Kubodin grinned. It was a typical attitude from a warrior of the hill tribes. And in the end, it was likely what would happen.

"It may be a trap though. The scouts could not get around that force to see what was behind it. We might engage it, or try to engage it, only to be lured toward a greater army behind."

Dakashul shook his head. "You think too much lately, Kubodin."

Maybe that was true, but Kubodin noticed that neither Dakashul nor the other chiefs actually said he was wrong about the possibility of a trap.

Tarok breathed deep of the smoky air. "Can we veer a little to the side, pass them by, and then head for Chatchek as we intended?"

"We can," Kubodin answered. "And maybe we should try that. But what message does it send our enemy, and our own soldiers, if we try to avoid a force very much smaller than our own?"

"It tells our enemies that we're weak," Sagadar said. The Night Walker Clan he was chief of were not renowned for bold action. That did not mean they were not brave though, and Kubodin did not underestimate them, or their chief.

"That is a signal we must not send," Kubodin told them. "We will therefore head straight for this force of riders. If they flee, as they must, we'll veer away rather than pursue them. I don't trust that it isn't some sort of trap, and the sooner we can reach Chatchek the happier I'll be."

He knew some of the others were not so keen on using a fortress. It was not their way of fighting, but Shar had convinced them to try it, and he himself had been there. If they had the time to refortify it before an enemy attacked them, it would be close to impenetrable. Except for sorcery.

The meeting broke up, and some of the chiefs drifted away to their own tents while those who remained began to talk of everyday events. Kubodin remained silent though, and his thoughts kept running back to Shar. Where was she now? Had she found the valley she sought? And most of all, when would he see her, and Asana, again?

It was a clear morning next day, and the sky had just lit up as Kubodin had a man sound the horn that signaled the day's march should begin. They went ahead in battle formation, with their cavalry forming a wedge at the front. Cavalry was the best way to fight cavalry, if it came to that.

Moreover, he headed straight at the enemy's last known position. They would not be in any doubt as to his intentions, but by their own behavior he would better be able to tell if they expected reinforcements to join them, or if indeed they were already close by and it was a trap.

The morning wore on. The men were nervous, as they always must be when facing battle. Only fools assumed that the deadly touch of a blade would pass them by and they would survive while others perished.

Frequent reports from the scouts came in. The force of a thousand riders had grown. It was two thousand now. Even so, it was no match for Shar's army, and Kubodin hastened ahead.

By noon, he drew close enough to see the enemy. He did not attack though. He picked an area of higher ground, a mile distant, and there he gave orders for the men to rest and eat a leisurely lunch. However, he kept a strong watch on the enemy and was ready for any attack.

No attack came, and it would have been folly of the enemy to try. Yet still, he wondered what their purpose was.

"Have they fortified Chatchek themselves, do you think?" He directed the question to Nahring, who was closest to him at that moment, the other chiefs only just returning from a tour of the soldiers to ensure morale was good.

"Maybe, but I doubt it. Shar is different from many of the Cheng, shamans and chiefs alike. Only *she* would come up with the idea of using a haunted fortress as a base for warriors who liked to fight in the open, get it over with in a day, and then go home. And only Shar could convince an entire army to go along with her plan, once she thought of it."

Kubodin laughed. "Very true! Yet still, what are they playing at out there?"

The enemy cavalry was not resting as Shar's army was. They had started upon their horses, but had dismounted when it became clear the approaching army stopped for a lunch break. It would vex them, for it showed that Kubodin treated them with contempt. He did not, but it looked that way, and that was what mattered.

"Maybe they're just concerned that we'll turn west and try to drive in toward Nagrak City," Nahring said.

Kubodin was not convinced. "That ruse is stale now. They might have thought so a few days ago, and that was Shar's plan, but it would not benefit us to delay that. The time we have spent coming up northward was time they had to better prepare their defenses. If we were going to attack, we would have done it by now and they know it."

Whatever was going on, it was time to call their bluff and press forward. The men were rested, and Shar's army far outnumbered the meagre opposition. He signaled for the lunch break to finish, and soon after they continued their march.

The enemy riders waited for them. If it were battle they wanted, they would get it. Kubodin hefted high his axe.

"We'll chase these pony riders away!" he called out. "They'll not stand and fight. Have at them!"

They were close to the enemy now, and he signaled his own cavalry to move out to the left flank of the Nagrak riders. At the same time, he ordered spearmen who had earlier been prepared to the front ranks. A cavalry charge might break Shar's army, but it was unlikely. A well-trained group such as these men were would hold their ground, and horses, even if their riders were stupid, were smart enough to turn around or shy away from a wall of spear tips. So long as the men held their nerve against the charge, at least, which was no easy thing.

When all was ready, he ordered the army into a rolling charge. It was not fast, but it would get them to the enemy more speedily if they had bowmen, which Kubodin could see no sign of but it was best to be prepared.

The enemy stood their ground, sitting proudly on their mounts. Yet at the last they turned as one and gracefully abandoned the field. They did not hasten, and Magrig, who led Shar's cavalry now, shadowed them briefly. It might be that a trap was set to destroy Shar's cavalry, for they were far outnumbered and the farther they drew away from their own army the greater the danger.

If so, Magrig did not fall for it. He shadowed them, but kept his distance. Likewise, he would not be drawn out more than a few hundred feet. He stayed his riders, and let the enemy withdraw.

"What was it all for?" Argash asked.

"To buy time, I think," Kubodin answered. "They did not, nor ever intended, to fight. They just hoped to slow us down, either by hesitating before committing to battle, or else by seeing if they could make us change our course."

"To what end though?"

Of that, Kubodin could not be sure. "None to our benefit, that's for sure."

He signaled the army to march again, and it pressed forward. The enemy riders kept a great distance between the two forces, but they were visible at all times. At least, until night fell. A careful watch was kept, for Kubodin expected some sort of harassing tactic during the night.

No attack came, however, and next morning the army hastened ahead. Word came back from the scouts that the fortress was close now, and there were no signs that it had been occupied against them or invested to prevent their own entry. At that, Kubodin sighed a breath of relief.

Later that afternoon, the army came within sight of it. The landscape had changed as they traveled. It was now one of rising chalk downs and beech trees.

However much the landscape had changed, the fortress had not since the last time Kubodin had been here, and he doubted it had even through the course of the last thousand years. It hulked before them, impressive, ominous, implacable as time itself. It was a relic of a forgotten age.

"What of the ghosts?" Dakashul murmured. "Do the stories not tell of them?"

Kubodin clapped the chief on the back, acting a moment like his old self.

"Hey! I wonder how well they fight?"

Dakashul did not laugh, and Kubodin could not blame him.

"Never mind. I'm pretty sure they were grand warriors. The fight they put up to try to hold the fortress was incredible. When we enter it, you'll see what I mean. But have no fear. Shar made her peace with them, and they'll not harm us. If anything, they're on our side."

He hoped all that was true.

They came to the ruined gate, and the chiefs marveled at it. Kubodin remembered how he had felt last time he was here, and that same sense of awe overtook him again. This was hallowed ground. Brave men had fought and died here, on both sides.

He turned to the army behind him. It was too vast for all but a fraction at the front to hear his words, but what he said would be passed on to all the others.

"This is a mighty fortress!" he cried. "Skilled workers built it long ago. Brave men defended it. A great warrior-emperor took it! That is all in the past. The future is ours now, and we will make one to match the past, courage for courage and emperor for emperor. For are we not born of those long-ago people? Is not Shar descended from Chen Fei?" He paused and studied the faces of the warriors in the front ranks. He knew he was reaching them. "Shar has made peace with the ghosts here," he continued. "But we will remember them and honor them, even as we hope those who come after us will honor and remember our deeds. For I tell you truly, history will be made in this place, and our actions will be the stuff of stories to last a thousand years."

They entered the fortress after that, filing through the great gateway, and it took a long time for all the army to get inside.

Kubodin wasted no time. He set men to the ramparts to guard them, and to the few areas where towers had fallen and an enemy might seek to gain entrance. Meanwhile, he set teams to work to clean away rubble and rebuild the ramparts where they were damaged. The workmanship would not match what the ancient builders had achieved, but it would suffice. At least if they had enough time to carry out the repairs. A day, maybe two, would be required.

When that work was underway he gave orders for the less, if only slightly less, important tasks. The ruined gate at the front must be repaired, and the old wells that supplied water to the fortress must be found and brought back into use. If there were problems with them, new ones would have to be dug, but that was unlikely.

Last of all, the massive barracks where the men would sleep and rest must be brought into order, and the tiled roofs, where they were damaged, fixed. This was far less important, but winter was coming on and doing so would keep the men healthy and happy. If the enemy besieged them, they must endure the cold, wet and wind outside while the soldiers of Shar's army would sleep under cover.

These tasks were carried out with speed. It was incredible what an army could achieve in a short period, and Kubodin was impressed. It occurred to him too, that as it was with an army so it was with a nation. Broken and fragmented into tribes as they were, the Cheng had not advanced and lived little above a subsistence level. Yet if they worked together and cooperated, there was nothing they could not accomplish.

His good mood was broken the next day though. Scouts reported the enemy was gathering and coming toward them.

16. A Terror of the Old World

Shulu felt good again, or at least as good as her ancient body allowed. Her strength had returned after the illness, and she walked with a sprightly step.

The grasslands and small woods supplied one of her lore with food. It was always there for those who knew where to look, and surviving in the wild was not difficult for her. It did slow her down though.

She crisscrossed the open lands, hiding from the sight of men. That too, was rarely difficult for someone with her skills, even in the open. Yet, just like foraging for food, it delayed her.

Even so, Nagrak City was close now. It was a sunny morning, which warmed the air quickly after a cold night. Avoiding people was becoming harder now, for vast as the Fields of Rah were, and well-populated as she knew them to be, by far the greatest concentration of villages was here. And the city itself was something special. It was a relic from another age, and it held tens of thousands and was nothing like the rest of the Cheng lands. It was almost like the empire of old.

Only Chen Fei did not rule here now. The shamans did, and if the village shamans accumulated wealth off the people, the higher hierarchy here had enough gold to glut the dragons of old who hoarded it and guarded it with fire and malice. Even, so some tales went, they ate it and it became the fire in their bellies.

Shulu slowed, navigating carefully through a narrow ravine that cut down the side of a long escarpment. It was cold here, and she shivered. It was fairly thick with trees, even if only in a narrow band, for it was a long grove of trees watered by a stream that leaped and plummeted down the steep drop.

Her descent was not even. At times the ravine leveled off in shelves, and here the small stream filled pools with stone bottoms that provided good drinking water. It was not the sort of place common on the Fields of Rah, but she liked it here and had discovered it long ago. It reminded her of mountains, even as there were flat-bottomed vales in the mountains that reminded her of the plains. Nature always held the seed of its opposite in the extremity even as light gave way to dark, yet even on the blackest night there were stars.

She was halfway down when she heard a noise from above. It was faint, and few would have heard it above the rush of water. Yet she had been waiting for it, though hoping not to hear it, and using a trick of her power as a shaman to enhance her senses.

There was no other sound, but she was not mistaken. Something had been following her for days, and it was gaining on her. She had never seen it, and all the traps she had set for it, snares of magic and sorceries of deceit, had not thrown it off the trail. It was a thing of magic itself.

She turned her mind once more to determining what it was, but as always she drew a blank. It had to be the hound that had pursued her in the Forest of Dreams. Except the creatures of that forest did not leave it.

It was strange. Not knowing what it was made her uneasy. Yet her strength had returned, and she was a match for most things that walked upon the earth, burrowed in the ground or flew through the air. Otherwise she would not have dared to enter the Forest of Dreams earlier, where a myriad of such creatures, ancient, magical and cruel lived.

She had thought that she would reach Nagrak City and be done with it, for whatever creature it was would not follow her there. Yet now it gained on her.

Did it know Nagrak City was close? Was that why it had sped up its pursuit? If it did, was it controlled by the shamans? That was possible, but doing so with ordinary creatures was difficult enough. She did not think the shamans had the power to do it with the sorts of things that dwelled in the Forest of Dreams though.

She could hasten her pace. She might still reach Nagrak City before it, and leave it, whatever it was, behind. But the land ahead would be full of villages and farmsteads. The shamans would leave them alone and pursue her to the exclusion of all else. But if it was some creature from the forest, then who knew what it might do roaming the land. It could kill, for food or for pleasure, such was the way with many of the denizens of the forest. And many warriors would die before killing it, or making it flee.

Her choice was made. She could not go on. Rather, she must see what this thing was, and destroy it if necessary. Her duty was to Shar, but it was also to the land. All the Cheng peoples were her charge, for even if the emperor was dead, she was still his shaman, and that had always been his directive. *Protect the land before you protect me. I am nothing without the people.*

She moved ahead carefully, looking for a place where she might wait. It did not take long to find somewhere suitable. Slipping silently into a stand of trees that grew thickly around a little pond on an outcropping shelf, she became a shadow like the others.

The music of the little stream came to her ear as it fell over a short waterfall, and she used her magic to take that sound and weave it around her in a spell of silence. It would mute any sound she made. Then she cast her mind into the moving shadows and dappled light beneath the trees and drew it over herself as a cloak, masking her appearance. Not yet done, she caught with her magic the earthy smell of leaf mold where the litter of the decades slowly turned to soil, and this she wafted around her to obscure the scent of humanity. And she waited, less detectable than a shadow beneath the roots of a mountain.

Even so, nothing happened. She neither heard nor saw anything out of place. The ravine was peaceful, yet with a flutter of her heart she realized it was silent. No bird called or flew. An ominous hush lay over everything, and even the babbling of the stream was quietened. Nature knew when something dangerous approached before the senses of a human ever did.

The minutes drifted by. Each one seemed endless. Perhaps a half hour had passed, and still there was nothing. Almost, she thought she had been mistaken and there was nothing there. She had not lived so long by ignoring her instincts though. Whatever it was, it was just cautious. Perhaps, somehow, despite all her precautions it sensed her with magic rather than the senses of eye, ear, or nose.

The hush deepened. It seemed to beat in her ears as a tempest, and then at last she saw something. It was in the ravine a hundred feet or so farther up, hidden in the deep shadows of trees. But there had been some movement, of that she was sure.

Then it emerged, but kept to the shadows and undergrowth as it picked its way down the steep descent, following close by the stream.

Whatever it was, it walked on two feet. That she could tell, but there was something unhuman about it. Almost she moved so that she could position herself to see better, but swiftly discarded the idea. Whatever it was surely had an inkling that she was there, despite her magic, and she did not wish to frighten it away. It might be a long time before another opportunity such as this came. If she did not kill it now, or send it fleeing back to the forest, perhaps the next time it would be waiting for her.

It came on a little further, hesitated, and then stooped to drink. For the first time she had a proper look at it. It was not stooping. Rather, it had gone down on four legs to dip its snout in the water. It was not human at all. It was a strange creature, covered in striped fur and with flashing teeth that could rend. It was like a cat that could walk as a man.

Hidden where she was, Shulu felt her blood go cold. Fear gripped her as she had seldom felt before. Her memory threw up the words of the master who had taught her long ago, before there was an emperor or a Cheng nation.

He had described to her creatures of the old world, and one he had only whispered its name. *Tagayah*. She had thought it might be the hound from the forest, but she could not have been more wrong. This thing must have come from the forest, but if she had known that even one tagayah had survived the Shadowed Wars, she would not have dared to tread those leafy aisles.

Even in her far off youth, the tagayah had been a legend. Many creatures like it had died in battle in the wars, and the few that had survived had hidden, but eventually been discovered and killed, no matter the cost. But somehow this thing had survived. Only in the Forest of Dreams could it have done so, but it was strong enough that it need not hide there. It could go where it pleased, for no warrior, no group of warriors, perhaps not even a group of shamans could kill it. It was a beast fashioned of magic for one purpose. To kill. It fought with intelligence as well as tooth and claw, and there was poison on tooth and claw that could not be cured. It killed swiftly, but with great agony.

The creature rose to two feet and pricked its ears. Then it looked straight at her.

17. A Frenzy of Madness

Shulu could not see the eyes of the tagayah properly, yet still the malice that was in its gaze smote her like a blow. Then it cried out in a harsh voice, and the sum of all woe and madness was in it. It was part shriek, part growl and all insanity.

If the silence had been deep before, it was profound now. No bird or animal that heard that call would reveal itself. The most terrible of animals, such as a wild bull, that knew no fear otherwise, would slink away to hide.

Shulu wanted to run. But there was no outrunning a beast such as this. She stood her ground and sought the calm of Heart of the Hurricane. It did not come to her.

The creature took a few steps closer. A sapling that was in its way it smashed with a blow of a paw, shredding the bark with its claws. Then the great teeth gnashed, chewing and rending the sapling in a frenzy of madness.

Without doubt, the tagayah was insane. It leaped ahead, now on four feet and now on two, swapping seamlessly between gaits. Then it stopped again, head tilted, and looked at her. It made another sound. It was like a deep grumble, finished with a hiss.

If the creature could laugh, perhaps that was what it was doing. Anything was possible with a being of the Old World, born of magic before the age of men and steel. It might talk, though not in any language Shulu would understand. Certainly it was intelligent.

She stepped slowly from her place of hiding, and the eyes of the creature followed her every movement. There was a clearing, and she walked into it and then stood still.

She would not go to it, but make it come to her. The more she saw it move, the better she might understand how to fight it.

She tried to remember what she had learned of its kind. There was little that she had not already thought of. Insane. Poisonous. Deadly. One other thing floated up to her mind from her far-off youth. *Once its blood is up, it has no fear of death. None.* So said her old master, and she wished she could remember more, but likely that was all he knew himself and had ever said.

The tagayah suddenly bounded toward her, then veered to the side. It smashed into sapling, spinning away and rolling. Now was the time for her to attack.

But she did not. Something was wrong. The creature was just a little too far away from her, and any magic she cast at it would be weakened. It was a trap. The tagayah was trying to lure her into attacking so that it might gauge the extent of her power and the types of magic she might use against it.

"You'll have to do better than that," she said softly.

The creature came to two feet, and its ears twitched. It would not have understood her words, but her meaning would have been clear. She had been smart enough to avoid its trap, and taunted it.

It went down on four legs again, growling and hissing. Then it snapped at the dead leaves that littered the ground, rolling among them like it was in a death-struggle with an enemy. Then swiftly it charged at her, and the speed of it was amazing.

Yet Shulu was ready. She had expected as much, if not the speed of the attack. She leaped to the side, fire dripping from her fingers and sent a blast at the tagayah.

She hit it square on, and it was flung away. Fire caught in its bristling fur. It hissed and spat, pawing the earth, but it was far enough away again that her magic was diffusing.

She stilled it, and narrowed her eyes and watched with patience.

It made that deep grumbling and hissing sound again that she thought was a laugh. Clearly, the creature was not in pain. Or if it were, it enjoyed it. She remembered something then, some final word from her master. *The creature feeds of its own anguish.*

She did not know what that meant. She thought she soon would though, and in the next few moments would learn more about the creature than anyone had known in millennia.

The tagayah charged again. Its fur bristled, and the thick ruff around its neck flared out, revealing a sickly blue-pink tinged skin beneath.

Shulu sent fire at it, but even as it was about to strike the creature dodged, bounding to the side and then bounding back again. It was quicker than she was, and then its great weight smashed into her. Her body could not withstand such an impact, yet she drew on her magic and let it shine forth from her like light from a lamp. It strengthened her frame, and the touch of her magic would hurt the creature, for like the light of the sun it burned even if it was not flame.

Even so, she was driven back and knocked to the ground. The creature was all over her, jaws snapping and paws scrabbling to try to disembowel her.

She held it off, just. Her arms were stretched before her, and her fingers sunk through the ruff and sought out the neck. Magic gave her strength, for not even a powerful warrior could hold the beast back by force of muscle.

The fetid breath of the tagayah played over her face, and the stench was nearly overpowering. Saliva sprayed over her as it worked its jaws, trying by turns to reach her throat and clamp around her wrist. Then her skin burned where the poison from its mouth touched her.

She summoned all her magic, and channeled it into her body. With a surge of strength and fire, she cast off the creature and sent it spinning away. Somehow she came to her feet, but already it was leaping at her again. She dodged to the side, sending a spurt of magic at it.

The tagayah tumbled away, and in that brief respite Shulu slipped into the small stand of trees where she had hidden before. It had been a mistake for her to face it in the open. It was too quick for her. The trees would slow it down and give her a better chance to strike it with magic.

She found a suitable spot, and though she had not taken her gaze off the enemy for more than a second or two, it was gone.

If fear had gripped her before, now it turned the blood in her body to ice. It was not gone, that she knew. This was a battle to the death, and it would not relent, nor would she. It would not give up, and nor would she. Insanity drove it, and it had no fear. The welfare of the land, and Shar, drove her *despite* her fear.

But she could not kill what she could not see.

Or could she? The creature was close. She knew that, but some magic was hiding it. Whence it drew its power, she did not know. The gods, perhaps, or some other force. But if it used magic, there were ways to reveal it, and in doing so she might launch an attack at it that it did not expect.

She muttered a few words. A prayer, some shamans would call it. Perhaps it was. Or perhaps the power was her own and not granted by a god. She did not know, nor care. All that mattered was that it worked.

With the words, she gestured, her hand describing a quick arc. A silvery light powdered the air, and everything was revealed by it like motes of dust in a bright beam of sunlight.

She saw it then. The tagayah was crouched low on all four legs, stalking toward her, its fur having changed color and looking like the leaf mold, an aura of magic surrounding it. Its eyes, the pupils slitted vertically, shone with dark malice.

They both acted at the same moment.

Shulu sent a thrust of fire at the creature. The creature leaped up at her throat. Again it smashed into her, knocking her back and tumbling down amid the trees. The fire burned it though, and this time it screamed, the sound a shrill roar so close to ears.

They rolled over the ground, thrashing and scrambling. Tooth and claw sought to rend flesh, and magic sought to burn to ashes.

Pain ripped through Shulu. Then worse. Somehow they had come to the pond at the center of the little grove, and suddenly she was below the surface. The weight of the tagayah bore down on her, pinning her, holding her there by force of power as well as weight.

It would be over in moments if she did not get out now. Her strength would not last without breath, and the tagayah would rip her throat out before she could drown. Her bony hands were still around its throat though, and instead of trying to cast the beast off her, she gripped tighter, her fingers burying themselves into the corded muscles beneath the ruff of fur.

Fire burned at her fingertips, narrowing like pins of light, and they penetrated deep into the flesh. Any other creature would already be dead, but the tagayah still bore down upon her, thrusting her deeper into the water.

Shulu could see nothing, and her strength was failing swiftly. Yet still she concentrated, sending pulse after pulse of magic through her fingers.

Suddenly the weight was gone from her, and the creature leaped back, pulling her from the water with it because of her death grip about its neck.

She flung the tagayah away, water streaming from her. Her chest heaved with the need for air, and her heart thudded loudly and unevenly. Above all those feelings however was another. Anger, pure and ferocious.

Her eyes flashed, and fire surged from her fingers. Again and again she struck, and the creature began to burn. The ruff around its neck was like a wreath of flame. The fur on its chest smoked and withered away, revealing the sickly skin beneath. This blistered and peeled away as the flesh beneath began to burn.

Yet the tagayah laughed again, and Shulu wondered if she could beat it before she died. For truly, she was as good as dead now. The claws of the beast had ripped her flesh. The poison burned, and she could feel it working through her.

Her anger rose to new heights. Now Shar must contend against her enemies without help. At least the kind of help she could give to the one she considered her granddaughter. Others must do that now, but who would love her as she did?

The tagayah found its balance again, despite the magic destroying it. It leaped once more for Shulu, and Shulu, now fearing death no more because it had already claimed her, leaped forward to meet it.

The two crashed together. Shulu was knocked back to the ground, yet her hands fasted on the creature's head this time rather than its neck. It sought to tear out her throat once more, and her fingers sought its eyes.

The world had disappeared. To Shulu, nothing else existed now save her desire to kill this thing. Her fingers crept over its head. The fires kept burning, and the fur was alight. That would not kill it though. But at last she found the eye sockets, and her fingers sunk in.

The fire of her magic burned, and the slitted eyes of the creature steamed. It did not relent though, despite what must be extreme pain. Rather, it intensified its efforts to kill her. So too it called out again in that strange way that seemed a laugh.

Shulu weakened. Even as she did so her fingers drove deeper, and suddenly the eyes began to boil around her fingers. The tagayah thrashed and squirmed, yet did not jump away as it might have done to save its own life.

An eternity it seemed they struggled, and Shulu repented of her life. She had not been a good person. Only Chen and Shar had brought out the best in her, and she had failed them both when their need for her was at its greatest.

One last great surge of power was left to her before she died, and she summoned it now. Whatever happened to her, this thing must not be allowed to walk freely over the land. It was a thing of utter evil, and the harm it would cause would be immense. She may have blinded it, but that would only make it more vicious, and it had magic to aid its senses.

Her fingers penetrated further into the sockets. The magic gushed from her bony hands, breaking through at last to the brain. The tagayah stiffened, screamed once and then slowly toppled to the side, dead at last.

Shulu withdrew her hands. They were clean of gore, for the magic that did not burn her burned all else away. She vomited momentarily, then staggered to her feet and looked upon her last foe. She had vanquished it. Yet it had done the same to her, only a little more slowly. Soon, she would join it in death.

Even as she watched the strange creature began to fade. It seemed to break apart and fall into the earth as though returning to some other place whence it came originally. Within the space of a few ragged breaths it was gone.

Shulu moved to the pond and drank. Blood covered her. Her limbs were weak and trembly. Pain racked every muscle. Death, when it came, would be a release.

"Come then!" she called out, and her voice was still strong. "Come, Death. Have I not cheated you long enough?"

She did not fear it now. It was close, and her time was come. She had lived, and she had seen the glory of the world and loved those who loved her in return. Life was not forever. But love was, and she was content.

She sat down, leaning against a tree. It would be soon now. There was no escape for her. Then she straightened her head and looked upward. There would be no escape, unless…

18. Hail, Brother!

Asana's cry rang in Shar's ears, but if they tried to make a stand they would die. There was only one hope for them, and it lay between the massive pillars of stone that rose high into the fog, their tops hidden by the gathering gloom of dusk and the vaporish air.

"No!" she replied. "Follow me!"

She leaped ahead. The ragtag trample of boots behind her told her that she was obeyed, and she was glad of that. They followed her commands, even if they did not understand. That loyalty now had a chance of saving their lives.

The pillars rose up ominously, and there was a menace about them greater by far than the poles with skulls. She knew what was trapped inside the stone, but even without that knowledge their appearance was sullen and brooding. No one would willingly walk beneath their shadow, still less pass close by at night.

Yet she hastened to the left pillar and cast fear from her mind. She knew what to do, and if she failed then death would be swift.

The fog was alive all about them with the shifting shapes of wolves and dogs. Yet they lurked and threatened rather than attacked. They did not yet number enough to strike out into the open and try to kill, and waited for others to arrive. The sounds of yelping came through the fog though, and the others that were not here yet were very close, and they answered the calls of those that were, which directed them to their quarry.

Shar held the Sword of Dawn in her hand, and though it glimmered with a strange light in response to the magic in the pillars, it was still hard to see.

She placed her other hand against the cold stone. It was clammy to touch, but she found what she was looking for. *Five feet high. In the center. A notch in the stone like a crack, but it is no crack. Rather, it is part of the artifice to hide the means of invoking the magic.* Thus were the words of Shulu, and they sprang now to Shar's mind and helped her at her need.

A wolf leaped in among her companions, but Asana dealt with it in a single blow. All around, others pressed in, coming out of the fog.

Shar placed the tip of her sword in the crack, and slid it home as though it were a scabbard. *Magic calls to magic*, Shulu had said. *Like calls to like.*

A thrum ran through her hand, but she did not let go of the hilt.

"Atanador, nathrill sevestam!" she cried, using the words of power that Shulu had taught her for such a purpose. They were not Cheng words though, and they felt strange on Shar's lips. She had never spoken them before, and only said them in the vault of her mind to retain the memory of them.

The massive pillars burst into light. A plume shot up from the tips, piercing the darkened heavens. It was not white. It was like white blended with a dark shimmer as though a thin veil of black cloth were passed between the light of the moon and the upward-glancing gaze that beheld it.

The wolves howled, and the hounds bayed in dismay. Shar did not blame them, for it was an eerie sight. Then light sparked to another set of pillars a mile away, lighting them up as though with a flash of lightening. Then onward it a raced until a ring was formed around the Valley of Nathradin. In but a moment the leaping light had come full circle and sprang atop the two pillars before Shar from the other side.

"Quickly!" Shar called out. "Through the pillars now! The way is open!"

Her companions leaped through into the fog on the other side. It was thick, and they were almost gone from view within a few steps despite the light. Shar crossed the threshold herself, and even as she was about to draw forth the sword and close the gateway of magic, a voice boomed up through the pillars as though coming from the earth itself.

"Hail, brother!"

With the voice, a figure appeared above both pillars, massive and towering like a fortress of stone.

"Hail, brother," rang the metallic voice from her swords that she had heard once before.

Then all light snuffed out. The figure was gone and silence settled suddenly and completely over the land like a vast blanket. Of the wolves and dogs there was no sound. They were still close, but they may as well have been on the other side of the starry void. For Shar and her companions stood now in an enchantment of time.

"What on earth or in hell was that?" Huigar asked, and by the little light that was now left in the gloom of dusk and fog, Shar could see that her bodyguard, and friend, was scared. And she was not easily one to be so, for she had a bold heart of courage.

"Let us sit down," Shar replied. "We're safe now, at least from the wolves and hounds, and the shamans who control them. I'll tell you all."

They dared not venture far in the fog for fear of getting separated or falling into some ravine or hole. But they soon found a place of flat ground and grass, even if it was moist, on which to sit and take their ease.

"The magic of my swords and the pillars have the same origin," Shar began.

"Shulu Gan," Radatan murmured.

"Yes. Shulu Gan. Taga Nashu, the grandmother who does not die, and many other names beside through the long history of our land. But just grandmother to me, for that is what she *is* to me, and it makes no difference that it's not by blood."

She gathered her thoughts and considered how best to explain this. Some of it, Asana knew, but not all. The others knew nothing, though perhaps they had heard echoes of the truth in stories.

"Shulu was a shaman. Once, she led that order. Now she hates them. Her motivations and actions, the very essence of all that she is, might best be described as complicated. She is the finest person that I know, and she has made sacrifices to protect the land she loves that would make the strongest of us quail. Even so, she can be harsh. She can make choices that I would not, that might seem cruel or even evil."

The darkness gathered deeply about them now, but it seemed a light emanated from the fog that swirled above, enough at least that they might see by, if barely.

"Shulu has a reputation," Asana said, "In both history and legend. She is not one that I would trifle with. Nor to follow blindly. Above all though, her love of the land is clear, and that she has a purpose, gifted by fate itself, to help the land in its hours of bleakest dread. Such a dark path, hemmed in by enemies, is a hard road to travel and not all choices would be the same as one who walks carefree beneath the blue sky."

He knew, then. He understood the magic, and he did not judge its use. Shar's heart went out to him. Not only did he know, but he now tried to pave the way for her with the others, hoping to make it easier for them to understand.

She nodded imperceptibly at the swordmaster by way of thanks, and continued.

"The Swords of Dawn and Dusk were forged by Shulu to fulfill a great need. Chen Fei required great magic to protect him from the shamans. It had to be a magic greater than their own, one that they did not understand and could not defeat. If it were of their own kind, they could subvert it."

She turned and pointed back toward where the pillars were, hidden now from view.

"It was the same for the enchantment of this valley. She might have been strong enough to kill the shamans she trapped in it. Certainly she wished to. Chen Fei pressed her along those lines, and he offered a small army to help her. Yet by foresight she did not. Though they had betrayed the emperor, they still railed against the other shamans. They should be punished for their crime, yet likewise they must be offered the chance to repent in the future. In short, they might be useful again one day."

Shar took a deep breath, and let it out slowly. "To trap these shamans required a magic above their own, just as the forging of the swords did. So the swords and the pillars, though entirely different in use and function, are the *same* magic. One that only she knew, for she was the greatest of the shamans, and she did not share all her secrets with those she led. And it is well for us that she did not."

"What was the magic?" Radatan asked.

"There are living beings entrapped in the swords and pillars. Creatures of magic. Creatures that are the brothers and sisters of the gods, but that walk in the shadows of evil and were cast out of this physical realm at the birthing of the world."

Huigar hissed. "Demons?"

"Yes. Demons. It was their voices you heard just now."

There was silence. No one spoke. The fog roiled around them, and though unseen the presence of the pillars, or that which was in them, pressed in from the dark and made them all think of the worlds beyond the physical and mortal.

"How is it even possible?" whispered Radatan.

"And even if possible, how could Shulu Gan dare such a deed?" asked Huigar.

They were good questions, and Shar did not really have the answers.

"The second question is easy," she said. "Shulu dared because it was what she felt she *must* do to preserve the land, and that which she loved. When choice is taken away, a person will do what is left, no matter the risks. And in her case, she has a heart that burns with courage bright as the sun in the sky."

"And the first?" Huigar asked.

"If I knew," Shar replied, "then our enemies would know as well, and would surely have used the same magic against us. So far as Shulu knew, the secret of the magic is hers alone, and she shares it with no one, myself included. But this much she revealed to me. The demons are trapped, but it is a prison they freely entered into. In the case of my swords, one of their rewards is the blood spilled by them, which in the time of my forefather ran as a river, and will in my time also. The demons revel in it, and the swords are *thirsty* for bloodshed."

"And the pillars?" Asana questioned.

"I don't know. The motivation would be similar, I guess, but when dealing with demons, or with Shulu, nothing is ever as clear as it may seem."

They all considered this revelation for a while.

Radatan leaned forward, hugging his knees where he sat on the ground.

"Why didn't you tell us earlier?"

"I wanted to. I tried to. But I was afraid you would think less of me and Shulu. After all, I carry the swords. I use them. I benefit from the demons inside. I feared you would judge me."

"Never!" Huigar answered instantly.

Radatan nodded silently.

"And you, Asana?" she asked.

"I? Well, it's not for me to judge. At least not Shulu and her reasons. As for you, I don't judge you because you carry the swords. I judge you by what you do and how you act. All else is meaningless. And I have never so far found any fault in you."

Those words hung in the air. The others did not notice, but Shar did. Asana knew that carrying the swords gave them opportunity to influence the wielder. They might be turned to evil. As it was with her, so it was with Kubodin and his axe, which Asana must have known for a long time. She hoped she was as strong as the little hillman, for he had never given any indication that he was falling under the sway of the axe.

It was more dangerous if the shadow of the swords fell over her though. Should she become emperor, her power was greater by far than Kubodin's. She could do untold damage to the Cheng nation, and unleash evil across the land to make even the shamans pale.

Asana changed the conversation after that, and she was grateful to him. She had no desire to dwell on the fact that the power of demons was all around them, and that though she strove to do good, and did in fact do good, it was partly by the power of evil. Let the philosophers decide the right and wrong of it all, if they claimed to be wiser than Shulu.

"Are we trapped in this valley now?" The swordmaster asked.

19. The Blessing of the Queen

Shulu used the trunk of the tree against which she leaned to help her stand.

Her mind raced. What she would attempt now she did for Shar and the land. She had lived long enough. Death did not frighten her, and perhaps she even welcomed it. It was a release from struggle. It offered tranquility. The toil of her life, often in secret and without reward, would be over.

The morning sun shone brightly. The music of the stream and the small falls was in her ear, and even the sweet calls of birds had returned since the tagayah was defeated.

She straightened. What would come next would not be easy, and it would certainly fail. Yet she had to try.

With a shaky voice, she began to chant, and if it was always uncertain in her mind what the true nature of magic was, it was not so here. This was a prayer, and in no other way could a god be summoned, especially she who was their queen.

Her voice strengthened. Magic ran through her body, reaching out to the pond. The water there gleamed and flickered in the dappled light. Three times she chanted, her voice growing in power as the magic took hold of her. Then the water began to ripple and seethe.

The spell was done. Her voice was stilled. All that remained now was to see if the goddess would answer her call.

A breeze blew, growing stronger. It bent over the tops of the trees and sighed in them like a song of another world.

Perhaps it was. Shulu often sensed she was on the verge of something else when she conversed with the gods. The wind seemed to whisper words. The earth muttered them. It was as if two worlds were overlayed into the one, and for a moment she could catch a glimpse of the other. It was the realm of the gods, but it was vague and veiled to mortal eyes.

The breeze stilled. The pond became motionless like glass, and all the more did it reflect the sun in the bright sky.

The light grew brighter and brighter. Shulu shielded her eyes, but it pierced them anyway. Golden white it was, and she soon found she did not need to shield her eyes at all. Bright as the light was, it did not hurt.

Shulu lowered her gaze and watched the center of the pond. The gods used bodies of water as gateways, at least where possible. It was an avenue between worlds, and this is where the goddess would appear, if she came.

And she did. The light flickered to a deeper golden hue, arcing from the sky in a radiant beam onto the surface of the pond, and then faded save for a shimmering nimbus. A goddess stood there, upon the water, towering twenty feet into the air.

She was clad in simple white, with a belt around her waist of chained gold and a circlet on her head of gold also, beaten into shape by exquisite skill, or fashioned by magic. Her long hair trailed behind her, ruffled by the breeze that blew again, but only around the goddess for the trees did not move. It was gold, but there was a shimmer to it that spoke of embers stirred in an old fire and coming to life again.

The horns, as they always did, made Shulu uneasy. Yet the gods often took semi-human and semi-animal forms, and in this case they curved back from her head graciously like those of a ram.

Shulu bowed, but not deep. She feared falling over if she did so. Pain racked her body, and her heart seemed to beat rapidly and then cease altogether at whiles. She had not long to live.

The gods would not help her. This was a forlorn hope, for they would not interfere in such matters. She had fought the tagayah and beaten it, but it had killed her too. That was her fate as they saw it, and even if they had the power to help, she did not think they would. If the gods acted thus, it would throw out the balance of the world. She could ask though. And when that failed, she could try to secure some aid for Shar.

"Greetings, Uhrum, queen of the gods. You have blessed me with your presence."

The goddess looked down, her green-gold eyes piercingly bright.

"You may dispense with the formalities, Shulu. I see your injuries, and the poison that entered your body through them. Speak quickly, for you have little time to live."

Shulu straightened. She would not appear to beg for this, even to a god.

"Then I will state my request, Uhrum. And I will accept your answer, whatever it be. As you can see, I am dying. Yet my task on this earth is not complete. Shar is not yet emperor, and until she is the shamans rule, and they rule for their own benefit and not that of the people. This has brought great woe to the land, and it will continue. I do not ask for myself, but I ask for Shar so I can help her, and in turn so she can help the land. Will you cure me of the poison of the tagayah?"

Uhrum considered her. "You know that it is not the place of the gods to interfere in these matters. Humans must fight for their own destinies. If the gods become involved, the balance of the world may shift and unleash chaos."

Shulu bowed her head a little, then looked back proudly at the goddess.

"This I accept, and it cannot be otherwise. Even so, when I am gone, will you help Shar? Without me, she faces a might of magic beyond her capacity to resist. The shamans draw on the power of the gods, and Shar does not. There is no balance there. So, I beseech you, intercede on her behalf. Give her some aid so that she may be able to fight with a chance of victory."

Uhrum seemed to grow in stature, for she rose now above the tops of the trees and her eyes flashed. Involuntarily, Shulu took a step back. She had angered a god by her impudence. If so, it was of no matter. She would dare more than that trifle to help Shar. She stepped forward again, and stood defiantly.

The goddess spoke, and there was anger in her voice. Even so, the words startled Shulu.

"I have seen Shar, and she may surprise even you. The eyes of the gods see deeper than mortal vision. There is a strength in her seldom seen even in a hundred generations of your kind. Yet she does need help, but I will not give it to her."

"Then you condemn her," Shulu said swiftly.

Uhrum smiled. "It is ever thus with your kind. Even the wisest of you does not listen. I said that I would not help her. Rather, I will help you."

Shulu felt her heart race even more. "How so?"

"Cast your mind back to what I stated earlier. The gods will not interfere, for that will disturb the balance of the world. So it should be. So it is ordered. Yet still, despite the prohibition, one of your kind has sought such intercession from a god, and that request has been granted. Think you that any tagayah yet roam the world? I tell you they do not. The last was killed in the conflict humanity calls the Shadowed Wars. The one that you fought was brought hither by a god. Brought hither from another world, and set on your trail to kill you."

The voice of the goddess changed. The anger that was in it before gave way now to dignified sternness. She spoke as a judge might speak, weighing the fate of those they presided over, and delivering a verdict.

"Because a god has transgressed, and given aid that should not be given, the balance of the world has shifted. I will restore it. I do not give you an advantage, however. I merely reestablish the situation as it was before the interference. Yet gladly do I do so, for you have served your kind well, and the gods, or some of them, recognize that."

Shulu could not be more surprised, and she did not trust herself to speak. She went down on bended knee to signify her appreciation. Or perhaps it was the poison working deeper into her and robbing her of the last of her strength. She was not sure which.

Uhrum leaned forward from her great height, and one of her arms, slender and graceful, yet the same size as the branches of the trees nearby, lowered toward her.

The great palm rested atop Shulu's head, and it was the first time she had been touched by a god. Once more she had that sense of different worlds, only it was more intense. All about her things looked the same, yet different. Everything was lit by an inner radiance, and everything she saw was clearer, while everything she heard was crisper. She felt that if a wren landed a mile away in a tree she would be able to both see and hear it.

Greatest of all though, was the sense of peace that came over her. Tranquility infused her body and drew out weariness, pain and poison.

"I bless you," Uhrum said, and the tops of the trees rustled with the breath of the goddess.

"I cleanse you," Uhrum said, and the surface of the pond grew so still as to reflect the sky perfectly.

"I give you strength," Uhrum said, and the earth itself seemed to thrum.

Shulu felt her power return, and the poison that was in her dissipated in a wicked green mist, which the goddess blew away with a sigh that seemed to dislike, yet accept, the evils of the earth.

The golden light intensified, and the world disappeared. There was only the touch of the god, and no thought or wish broke that bliss.

Until the goddess slowly withdrew her hand. Then Shulu came back to herself, and realized she now lay on the ground. She stood, and she did so with vigor. She was not tired any more. She was not injured. She felt stronger than she had in a hundred years.

Uhrum stood just as she had before, her hands by her sides now. Her face was inscrutable.

Shulu could find no words, but she bowed deeply.

"You have served me well, daughter of the gods," Uhrum said. It was a term used of old, before even the reign of the shamans, to mark those priestesses favored by the gods. "Know these things. I have healed you, but the shadow of the tagayah will always be upon you. Once touched by madness, you will not forget it, and it will haunt your dreams from time to time. Know this also. Shar is not helpless, even against magic. And I do not talk of the swords you forged. Even now she is on a quest to free those shamans you imprisoned in the valley your kind name Nathradin."

Shulu felt the peace that had enveloped her before disperse, and dread replaced it. Those imprisoned shamans would likely kill her. Shar knew that, yet still some necessity had driven her to risk it.

"Be well, daughter of the gods," Uhrum spoke, and like a bolt of lightning, only surging upward rather than down, she arced into the heavens.

Shulu took a deep breath. What should she do now? Continue with her plan, or head for Shar as fast as she could?

20. The Witch-healer

Shulu drank from the pond, and she washed herself as best she could. Her clothes were torn in places and bloodstained, yet on her skin no injury from the tagayah was apparent.

It was time to leave here. Something terrible had happened in this place, and something exhilarating and tranquil. The first she would try to forget, and the second she would take with her. Whatever the case. It was time to go.

She followed the course of the ravine, passing by the small falls and twisting and turning her way downward just as did the brook. At length though, she came to its end.

The land was flat again. Trees and woods were few, and on the fertile grasslands were herds of cattle. She saw no sign of Nagrak riders, but they would be close. Where cattle were, riders were close by.

She stood there for a little while. A sense of urgency drove her, for she knew that time was precious. Yet what should she do? She could continue with her plan, and head to Nagrak City. There was much she could do there to hinder the shamans, and it was a good plan.

But Shar's need called out to her over the intervening leagues. She required help, and the help in particular of a shaman. Shulu knew she could give that to her, and then there would be no need to risk Nathradin.

Even if she decided to do that though, she would probably not reach Shar in time. And Shar knew better than she her needs and wants. She knew the risks of Nathradin too, and though willing to take great risks at need she was not foolish. She would not have begun that quest unless she had a plan that might succeed.

Her old arguments came back on her too, and suppressed her emotional urge to help Shar immediately. She yearned to go, but it was not the course of wisdom. It would only put Shar in even more danger, in the end. Better to split their forces, and give the shamans two enemies to fear, acting independently.

Besides, there was still the statuette that Asana carried, and he was still with Shar. The spell on that statuette was intricate, and had cost her much. Going to Shar now would work against that. Foresight was on her when she conceived that plan, and she would not second guess it now.

Her decision made, she strode out over the Fields of Rah with confidence. It was not her way to equivocate, and it felt good to have made a final decision and to stick to it. For Shar, she had done all she could. Directly, anyway. What she did now would be just as important, if indirect.

Nagrak City was not that far away now. The time of hiding was over. At least, she would substitute disappearing in the vast wild for hiding in plain sight beneath the very noses of her enemies.

Soon, she saw the smoke of a village plume lazily into the sky. It was time to assume her new identity, one the shamans would struggle to penetrate, as they always had through the centuries. She would become a witch-healer, for she had the skill, was an old woman, and throughout the land there were countless wandering old women who earned their dinner plying their skills with herbs and a touch of magic to cure toothache, tend injuries and soothe maladies.

Shulu changed direction slightly so that she headed straight toward the village, and put the shaft of a feather through her hood, one of the marks that people might recognize her as a witch-healer. Soon, she was on a path beaten by many feet before her.

The sun climbed higher in the sky, and beat down brightly. Despite that, the air remained chill. She pulled her hood up over her head as a group of riders trotted toward her from the village. To them, hopefully, she would just be any old woman, unless they had orders to question every old woman they saw.

The riders approached. Their ponies looked fresh, and the warriors rode them expertly. They were all old men though, and that told Shulu that the younger warriors had likely already left the village, and others like it all through the Fields of Rah, to mass into an army.

When they were close, Shulu addressed them. Better to speak first, rather than give the impression she did not want to interact with them, which would be suspicious.

"What news?" she called out, adopting a slight change to her voice and replicating the accent of these people.

The riders pulled up, and their leader studied her while his pony kept shifting its footing to disturb flies annoying it.

"War is coming. You'll have opportunity to ply your healing skills soon enough."

"Not here though, surely?"

The rider laughed. "Not here, old mother. You're safe. But warriors will return soon enough, and many will be wounded. You and your kind will be busy for a long while to come."

Shulu peered up at him, drawing a mask of anxiety over her features.

"We'll win though, won't we?"

"Of course. Rest easy. Word is we're going to hit the army of this supposed descendent of the emperor hard. It'll all be over by winter."

"Is she really a descendent of the emperor?"

The man looked suddenly wary. Perhaps he wondered if she were a spy for the shamans, and if word of anything he said would be reported back to them.

He shrugged. "So the rumors say. I'm just a cattle herder, so I know nothing. Nothing, except her army will soon be defeated."

Shulu bowed to him. "Thank you for your time, young man."

She had learned something useful. He had said all that he would be expected to say by the shamans, especially that Shar's army would be defeated, and soon. What he had not said though was that Shar *herself* would be defeated. She might be reading too much into it, but it seemed to her that secretly her defeat was not something he was hoping for, otherwise he would have aimed his comments at her specifically. Even among the Nagraks, which was a stronghold of the shamans, there were those who might support Shar if given freedom to do so.

The riders kicked their ponies into a trot, and soon were some distance away. Shulu continued toward the village, but she did so thoughtfully.

It was not that long before she reached the outskirts, and there she found a cattle market. There were several sets of yards, each filled with oxen. No doubt the riders she had met had driven their own stock here to sell.

The smell of the yards drifted to her, and she liked it. It was not altogether unpleasant, and it reminded her of her youth. Once, a very long time ago, she had been a farm girl. She wished for the joy and simplicity of it again, for it brought peace and tranquility. That life was denied her though. She sighed, and walked on.

It was a fair sized village. The perimeter was surrounded by a timber palisade, as many villages all over the land were. It was a sign that raids were not that uncommon, but this deep in Nagrak territory it signified that Nagraks sometimes raided other Nagraks, rather than that these people feared a raid by a more distant tribe.

She walked down the main street, the dust having been settled by a passing shower during the night that Shulu had not experienced outside on the grasslands.

"Witch-healer!" someone called.

It was a middle-aged woman, her hands rough from labor.

"What is it, child?"

"My husband is sick. Will you come and see him?"

Shulu had not expected to be called upon so soon, but if she wore the feather she must answer the call.

"Of course. Show me the way."

The other woman hesitated. "We don't have much to pay you."

"Never mind dear. Whatever you have will be enough."

A look of gratitude passed over the woman's face, and then she led the way. She spoke little, and Shulu was content with that. She was too old to listen to people prattle.

They came to a hut several streets over, near the palisade. It was dark inside, and the smell of smoke was in it.

"Husband, I found a healer for you."

A figure stirred on the floor, turning over several animal skins that served as blankets.

"It's my toe," a man said. "Can you help?"

"Maybe. We'll see." She turned to the wife. "First, let's get some fresh air in here. The smoke and the dark are unhealthy."

The woman pulled back the cowhide door that blocked the entrance, and held it in place with a leather thong tied to a nail. Then she went to the other side of the hut. There was a window there of similar fashion, only smaller. It was not much, but it would get a cross breeze going, and admit a little more light.

"Keep both door and window open as often as weather allows." Shulu said. "Fresh air is healing. Old air causes illness."

She squatted down to examine the man. "Which toe is it?"

"It's the big toe on my right foot."

Shulu could see the problem straight away. The toe was swollen and red.

"Did the attack come on suddenly?"

"Just last night it started," the wife answered for the husband.

"Have you had an attack like this before?"

"I have. It lasted a few days, and then got better. Can you cure me?"

"Do you drink beer?"

"He drinks beer!" his wife answered for him again. "Too much if you ask me."

Shulu understood the wife's concern. Probably she drank it herself though as well. It was not beer that was the problem though. It was people not knowing when to *stop* drinking it.

"And do you eat organ meats such as liver?"

"Of course," the man replied.

Shulu gently brushed her fingers against the man's toe. He flinched despite the lightness of her touch, and she felt warmth of the skin.

"You have a condition known as gout," she said.

"The gout!" the wife said. "I thought so. My uncle had that real bad when I was a child."

The man looked up at Shulu, a pleading look on his face. Gout was painful, and he wanted her to help desperately.

"I can relive the pain, somewhat," Shulu said. "But know that the cause of the ailment is drinking too much beer and eating offal. Cease to do both until the pain is completely gone. Then, you may have one mug of beer a day, if you want it. But eat no more offal. Ever."

She produced some dry herbs from within the inner pockets of her cloak. Her store was very low, and she would have to find, or buy some, shortly. She gave the herbs to the wife.

"Make a tea out of this three times a day. There's enough there to last two days. By then, he should be well enough to walk around again."

She turned back to her patient. "This will hurt a little at first, but then the pain will dull. Between this and the herbs, you should feel well. Yet I urge you to rest for two days, as much as possible. And don't be deceived by the pain going. The gout will come back on you if drink too much beer or eat too much offal. Do you understand?"

"I promise," the man said. "I'll do as you say."

Shulu was not convinced. In her experience, those who suffered such maladies went back to their old habits within a few weeks of the pain subsiding. Until the next attack, of course.

She rubbed her hands together briskly, then clapped them three times. The clapping was useless, but over the long years she had found that some conspicuous gesture had a greater impression on the patient, and they were more likely to believe in the treatment. And that belief helped the treatment.

Muttering a few words, part nonsense and part spell, she placed her palm over the toe and let a tendril of magic unfurl. It eased through the man's flesh, and then she directed it to the joint. The man groaned in pain, but to his credit did not move. It was a good sign. He believed in her skill as a healer.

She used the magic to open the joint slightly, and take away some of the heat. The skin was immediately cooler to the touch, and already some of the swelling was reduced.

She took her hands away and clapped three more times. It was unnecessary now, for the remedy she had just administered had impact enough.

The man let out a cry of joy, and he smiled broadly enough that it seemed his face might crack.

"Witch-healer, you're the best I've ever seen. The pain is gone. Gone!"

He was about to spring up off the floor, but Shulu cautioned him.

"Take things easy. Walk a little bit, but only gently. If you walk far or do hard work, you'll bring it back on."

"I'll do just as you say," he answered. He stood slowly, and tested his weight on the foot. All seemed to be well.

"And remember," Shulu said. "Only small amounts of beer, and no offal."

His wife gave him the tea she had prepared, and she gestured Shulu to sit down at the small table.

"Like I said, we don't have much, but I can repay you with a nice meal."

"A meal will be fine," Shulu replied. In truth, she was getting hungry and had little use for coin. She carried enough on her already, and her agents in Nagrak City would provide her with more.

The wife went over to the hearth and fussed over a pot suspended above it by a chain. Then she retrieved a bowl, broke some bread into it and spooned something from the pot into the bowl, serving it to Shulu with a smile.

It was a stew of some kind, either of beef or horse. Whatever the source of the meat, there was not much but the broth was good and the bread was fresh. It tasted good, and Shulu ate it with relish.

"Would you like some more?"

Shulu nearly said yes, but neither the husband nor wife had joined her in the meal, for food was likely scarce.

"No, that was plenty, thank you. And very nice too. Perhaps I could trouble you for some water."

"Of course!"

While the wife found a mug and poured water from a large earthenware jug into it, Shulu turned her attention to the husband.

"What news with the war? I hear it will be over before winter."

The man rubbed his face. "So our shaman tells us. But there's not a warrior of fighting age left in the village, nor in any village for miles and miles around, so the rumor goes. If this Shar Fei is so easy to beat, what need do they have of all our men? It's the older folk such as me that are left herding the cattle and tending the fields. And hard work it is too."

Shulu let the subject drop. She did not want to be conspicuous, and already she might be because the cure she worked was better than any regular witch-healer, or even shaman, could accomplish.

She wandered through the streets after that, and spent a few copper coins on new clothes, and the purchase of some supplies, including herbs. Then, as the afternoon was coming on, she made the choice to spend the night in the village. She was not much of a talker, except to Shar, but traveling through the wild lands was lonely. It would be good to be surrounded by people again, even if she only heard them and did not speak to them.

By nightfall, she had found a barn that housed goats, and she bedded down in the straw. The owner was wealthier than most in the village, and had looked at her with disdain and overcharged for the privilege of sleeping in an outbuilding. It was of no importance though. Soon, very soon, Shulu would enter Nagrak City for the first time in a thousand years. As she dreamed that night, she did so of the city, and the people and times she had once known in it.

21. Nagrak City

Shulu woke next morning, and she was not particularly refreshed. Dreams had troubled her all night.

The gray of dawn peeped through cracks in the barn door, and she decided to make a swift exit. She had not liked the owner, and wanted to avoid talking to her, which she would surely have to do soon when the goats were milked.

She left, and soon was on the main street again. She was not the first riser, and she met others who greeted her. They were friendly, as most Cheng were of any tribe. So long as you were not a warrior in a strange land. Women and merchants passed freely everywhere.

The sun rose properly as she left through a gate in the palisade. It was open and unguarded, which was just as well. The less questions she faced the better.

The path was well beaten for a mile or so, then it faded away. She saw quite a few other travelers, most farmers bringing produce into the village. She saw no warriors, and that was good for her but bad for Shar. It was clear that the entire Nagrak Tribe was mobilized for war.

The situation was not a surprise. The shamans had underestimated Shar, or overestimated themselves, but now they would spare no effort to destroy her army. If they could.

By mid-morning she could see Nagrak City ahead. It was just a smudge on the horizon, and she could see nothing clearly. Part of the reason for that was the distance. The other part was the great amount of smoke that hung above and around it. The city was huge, and the number of cooking fires was vast.

The grasslands around her were near bare of trees. Once, there had been more. The demand for firewood had outstripped any forest growth by far though, and now much was imported. At least for the wealthier households. The poorer made do by burning dried dung.

As afternoon drew on, she came closer. She could see the wall now, and it gleamed white. The stone was covered by a mixture of chalk, clay and resins every so often. She wondered how they had kept that tradition alive. It was not easy, and it did not last long, especially in rainy decades.

Chen Fei had started it, and for good reason. It was an impressive sight, which was something that every capital city should aspire to. It gave the inhabitants pride, and awed visitors from other countries. With a grimace, she realized that likely the money for it came from taxes that would better be spent on help for the poor. In Chen Fei's time, the poor were helped first, and other needs met afterward. With the shamans, they *wanted* people to be poor. That, and indoctrinating youth through what limited education they received, was a means of subtly subjugating them.

The wooden palisades often seen in villages in the Fields of Rah were an imitation of this, and often painted white too. But the original was truly a remarkable sight, especially on a sunny day.

Above the wall she could see the steep-roofed and many-tiered pagodas soaring toward the sky. The tiles gleamed red, and contrasted with the walls. Some were black, coated in paint to be such, and others were enameled green. How well she remembered those towers, and the cool night breezes in summer at their tops beneath the stars. She tasted the plum wine now on her lips, and the cool drinks of crushed ice and squeezed juices. How far the empire had fallen since then. How deep the sin of the shamans to hold it back by fostering tribal antagonism so as to keep power concentrated among themselves.

Their time was coming. For every evil there was a reckoning. At least, if Shar lived long enough.

She trod a path now between farms of plum trees, the leaves falling to the ground at each breath of wind. They were about to go dormant, but she knew how glorious they looked in the spring, their countless blossoms like snow drops. She remembered that too, and the hum of bees in the air and the joy of spring in the city.

It would not be possible to go on like this. Chen Fei was gone, the past was dead, and the empire was no more than a dream. If it were to become reality again, she must concentrate on the task at hand.

The path she followed developed into a road, and that road soon joined a highway, lined with stones. No farmer's cart would get bogged here in the wet season.

Nagrak City was close now, and she prepared herself to enter. There would be guards at the gate, and likely they would be on watch against spies from Shar's army. And maybe even her. Although it was possible that they thought she was dead now, killed by the tagayah. They had no way to discover otherwise.

The mighty gate was before her now. She hastened to come up close behind a group of farmers, hoping the guards would pay her less attention when they had just been busy. That hope seemed to fail, though. The guards questioned each farmer closely, and their carts were searched. They would give her due scrutiny as well.

At length the farmers were ushered through in turn, and she presented herself to the guards, hood down but the feather signifying her trade still visible.

"What's your business in the city, woman?"

"I'm a witch-healer, as you can see," she said, touching the feather.

"What of it? The city has more than enough of your kind. You'll not get much work here."

Shulu hid her irritation and bobbed her head. "I'll take what work I can get. I have a reputation here, and I think my cures in the past will earn me a few chances. Sick people remember those who healed them, and recommend them to their friends."

"What tribe are you from? You don't sound Nagrak to me."

Shulu grinned at the guard. This was a trick question, intended to make an infiltrator appear nervous, for she knew her accent was accurate. He was clearly looking for spies, which was good. He did not seem to have any suspicions of old women, and that was even better. The shamans thought her dead, or did not guess she would come here.

"Now listen here, young man. I'm a Nagrak. I lived here long before you were born. I know this land, and this city, better than you, and I can tell from your own accent that you come from the west of the Fields of Rah, probably from the Nightbringer Canyons, and your parents likely raised goats instead of horses because that's what they do in the canyons. Now, if you want to make me angry young man, tell me I don't sound like a Nagrak again!"

The guard looked stunned, and his fellows laughed at his discomfort. He waved her on with a gesture, but even as she was passing through the gate he called out to her.

"You're right! I *am* from the Nightbringer Canyons, and I prefer goats to horses!"

Shulu laughed at that. "Goats aren't so noble as a horse, but they're better company. You won't win many friends in the city saying that though, so I'd keep that opinion just between you and me."

She walked on then into the city. Her heart was lighter than it had been for a long time, and she hummed a tune to herself as she strode ahead. Then she stopped humming. It was an old tune that had come into her head, and likely had not been heard for hundreds of years. If the wrong ears, belonging to a shaman with longevity magic happened to hear her, he would be suspicious. Small mistakes could be costly.

The streets were crowded. She had forgotten what it was like to be in a place that teemed with thousands and thousands of faces, and every one of them a stranger. She did not like it, and preferred life in a small village. The peace and quiet was better for the soul. The tranquility was a balm.

As it was with the sights, so it was with the sounds. Noise came from every direction. Hawkers yelled out, vying for attention against others to sell their goods. Shop owners called from their doorways, and everywhere was the sound of talking, laughing, arguing and the tread of boots against the cobbled streets. She hated it. And she loved it.

The crowds unnerved her, for it had been so long since she had been among ones like this, but it pleased her too. Should she be discovered, she could easily slip away and hide in the multitude. The streets themselves were a good place to hide, for nobody could pay attention to all the people there, but she had a better idea than that in mind.

She walked ahead, looking at buildings and pagodas that once she would have known by sight, but now they all seemed the same to her. Even so, her feet knew which direction to take, and she chose streets and lanes that led her to her destination.

It was not easy to pick out individual conversations as she walked among all these people, but she listened to the gossip as best she could. Shar's name came up over and over again.

Some feared Shar's army. Some scoffed, saying it would all be over in a month. Some raised their hands and gestured bewilderment if someone asked them what was going to happen. That was likely the most accurate response, for Shulu did not know herself, and nor did the shamans. This was a rebellion such as the shamans had not faced in a thousand years, and no one knew how it was going to end.

No one said they liked Shar, or what she was doing. But many were silent on the issue, or gave a minimal response. It was the quiet ones that Shulu was interested in, for it would be to risk your life in a city controlled by the shamans to show any support. As far as she could tell, about half the population here might well be secretly on her side. That was not a bad amount, considering Nagrak City was swamped with shamans, and they had controlled it as the center of political power since murdering Chen Fei. It was easier to stamp out opposition in a place such as this than in rural areas.

She passed into the inner-city as the afternoon was waning. The lanes and streets were deep in shadows at times, but the quality of the housing was even better. There were no wooden buildings here. All was of stone or brick, and much of it was grand. This was an area where the nobles lived, close to the palace in the center of the city. The yards were large, and often decorated with elaborate gardens, fountains and statues. At least as far as she could see. Most of the residences were walled, once more with whitened stones to imitate the city rampart.

No wall had kept her out though, and she grinned to herself. And if the time came, Shar knew how to besiege a city such as this, and penetrate that defense.

Shulu avoided the palace, traveling farther than she needed to in order to ensure she did not see it. There were too many memories for her there.

At length, she walked down a street that she knew. It was a grand promenade, and the houses here had not changed greatly. There were some newer ones and these she recognized by their inferior construction, but the older ones were as she remembered them.

Her destination was not one that she knew though. It was an older mansion, though perhaps not from Chen's time. A great oak grew in the front yard, ancient and hoary. Its leaves were beginning to drop, yet the grass beneath was immaculate. Here, she stopped and studied it a moment, gathering her courage. What she was about to attempt came with great risk.

After a few moments, she shrugged and walked through the gate, which was open, and along a stone path that led beneath the oak and drew to a stop at the mansion's front door.

The door was old, and the knocker was of bronze, fashioned as the head of a horse. She hesitated but a moment, then forcefully used the knocker, striking three times.

Momentarily, the door opened and a manservant appeared, his livery black with gold trimmings. He looked her up and down, and then spoke disdainfully.

"What do you wish, woman?"

"Employment."

"There are no vacancies." The servant began to close the door, but Shulu quickly placed her foot in the way.

"Your master will have a vacancy for such as I. Fetch him. Tell him I'm a witch-healer of the highest skill, and that I know what he does. I can help."

The servant looked indecisive. "Fetch him," Shulu persisted. "Otherwise, when he discovers someone else has hired the talent you turned away, you'll be looking for a job yourself."

The servant said nothing. A few moments he looked at her, then opened the door and let her in. He gestured for her to sit in a parlor to the left of a grand hallway, and there she waited while he disappeared, his footsteps soon fading on the marble floor.

Shulu sat and thought of anything but the task at hand. It was dangerous, and the one she would see might detect subterfuge if she were not careful. She must *become* the witch-healer she claimed to be, in every word she spoke.

She looked around. Just this waiting room was larger than most chief's huts across the land, and the antique furniture in it, lacquered and polished to a gleam, was worth more in gold than the entire wealth of a small village.

It took some time, but eventually she heard footsteps approaching. There were two people this time, and soon the master of the house appeared, the servant a pace behind him.

They came into the room, and Shulu stood and curtsied.

The master of the house looked at her sternly. He was dressed in black robes and a cowl, which he still wore up even indoors. Gold rings glittered on his fingers, but his eyes were cold. She knew him for what he was: a shaman of the worst sort, and a powerful one, but not yet admitted to the ranks of the elders.

"What do you want, woman?"

"Your servant will have told you. He will also have told you of my claim to great skill. I know you train nazram, and I know many are injured in the arduous training. I can heal them better and faster than anyone you have working for you. And that will save you money. In short, I'm the best healer you'll ever see, and you have need of me."

He laughed at that, and she held her anger in check. It had no place here.

"Test me," she said.

He looked like he was about to refuse, and then changed his mind abruptly.

"Very well. Follow me, I have an injured man. If you can heal him, then I'll employ you."

The shaman dismissed his servant, and led her through the mansion. If the parlor where she had waited showed signs of wealth, it was as nothing compared to this. Shulu allowed herself to show signs of being impressed. That would help ease any suspicion against her, and she set her mind to healing this wounded man. Once she did that, then she *would* be employed here, and there was no better place for her to hide. No one would expect Shulu Gan to work for a shaman and to conceal herself beneath their very noses.

More than that, she would be able to gather information from the nazram trainers, perhaps his friends, and monitor what the shamans were doing. She had spies in other mansions like this, doing the same thing, but it was only by gathering bits and pieces of information from all over that she could build a true picture of what the shamans planned. The more sources of information, the better.

They exited the mansion at its back, and walked through a massive training area covered in sand where warriors sparred and trained under the supervision of instructors. Going beyond this, they entered a much less grand building that served as some kind of barracks. It was austere in here, although it would be luxurious to warriors from villages that came here for training. At length, they came to a room where a number of people were gathered, including a witch-healer.

Yet when Shulu saw the injured man on the bed, the center of all attention, her heart sank.

22. The Fear of Magic

Kubodin stood upon the ramparts of Chatchek fortress, and he marveled at how quickly the damaged areas had been repaired. Nahring was with him, but their gazes were drawn away from the fortress to the ground below.

An army had gathered there. The enemy that had threatened had at last come. For every man he had, they had two, and still it was but the first stirring of the wave that might come against them.

"Tell me, Nahring," he said. "Do the men still wish to fight in the open? Or do they feel better about Shar's choice to use a fortress?"

There was a moment's silence, then Nahring answered quietly.

"Shar is wiser than anyone her age should be. Without this fortress to stand between them and us, then I fear even brave men might have surrendered or fled by now. And those with even greater courage would already be dead on a battlefield, the war, such as it was, already over."

There was truth to those words. "Shar is Shar. She's had the benefit of instruction all her life from Shulu Gan. Even so, a potter may fashion a clay vessel, but it's the fire that makes it. Or a smith a sword, and there too, despite the smith's skill, it's the fire that tempers the steel. Shar is who she is because that is her."

Nahring turned his gaze away from the enemy and at Kubodin.

"Do you mean then that this, this war, is the fire that will temper her?"

"It will be so. Look beyond this war to when she is emperor. She is remarkable now. When she wins, as I think she will, then will she not be such a leader as this nation needs? The people will gather to her as our army has, and the empire that once was will rise in glory again."

Nahring gave no answer. Instead, he looked back at the enemy. It was fine to speak of the future, but right now it was hard to believe in one when an army had come in vast numbers to snuff it out.

With a cool gaze, Kubodin took to studying them again. They were Nagraks, nearly to a man. It was hard to be sure, but at least all those who had come close to the wall were, which only made sense. The Nagraks were a vast tribe, and the closest. Still, there were tribe after tribe behind them to the west. What if the shamans mobilized them all? Did Shar have a plan for that?

Even as he watched, he saw that preparations were underway for an attack. A mass of the enemy separated, and several shamans led them. Drums began to beat, and then the force rolled forward. So many were they that the sound of their rolling march was as thunder.

"The walls don't seem so bad now, hey?" Kubodin said, falling back into his old self and the way he used to speak.

"Not so bad at all," Nahring said, drawing his sword.

The enemy rushed on. From the ramparts volley after volley of arrows fell, thickening the sky. It was not enough, yet at Shar's instructions he had recruited a lot more bowmen, had them trained, if swiftly, and set aside work teams to construct the bows and arrows. Clearly, he needed to do even more of that.

After the arrows came the spears. These, like the arrows, killed many of the attackers, but not enough. They hit the walls as a wave crashes into a seaside cliff, and then they threw up their ladders and grappling hooks.

Again, he had trained men for this. They swooped in, dislodging ladders, cutting grappling hooks and sending men toppling to death or injury.

The enemy fled back to the safety of their main army, and for some of the way they were pursued by more death from the sky.

Kubodin had not drawn his axe. He held himself in reserve against an attack by shamans, but they too fled back with the soldiers. They dared not use sorcery yet. But if they were repelled again and again, they would resort to it no matter the traditions of the Cheng people.

He beckoned two men over. They were older warriors, and captains of squadrons.

"You," he said, gesturing to the first. "Take your men through the gates and gather as many spears and arrows as you can. We'll need them. Hurry, lest they attack again and force you back inside." He had not realized just how precious a commodity spears and arrows were. It was a mistake, and one that he did not think Shar would have made.

He looked to the second man. "Take your men and go to the workshops. Help in any way possible with the construction of bows, arrows and spears. And send hunters into the forests above Chatchek to secure as much of the right sort of wood as possible."

So far, the enemy had not surrounded the fortress. The front was accessible to them, but the sides and rear backed onto steep country and cliffs that were difficult to traverse. Especially for an army, and one that would be attacked if they tried for he had set regiments there to prevent it.

The supply lines had shifted too, and now came down from the rugged hills at the back of the fortress from paths that hugged the north coast. A mass of supplies arrived every day, both food and equipment. He was gathering a great supply, and he would need it for a siege. Sooner or later the enemy would succeed in surrounding them and would cut off all outside help. Then the squeeze would really begin.

They had been lucky with water though. Even when they ran out of food they would not go thirsty. Whoever had built this fortress in ages past had positioned it cunningly, and the ancient wells still ran deep with sweet water.

The gate had been difficult to fix. The metal had been tortured by fire and battering rams in its youth and left to lie for a thousand summers beneath heat and rain, and a thousand winters where cold and ice worked upon it. Despite such travails, that would have ruined ordinary iron, it was still strong. There was magic in its making though, and it had resisted everything that time and war had thrown at it. Now, it had come back to its former glory within a furnace and beneath determined hammers. It would bar the way of another enemy once more.

Longest to restore had been the ramparts, where they had fallen into disrepair. No great skill was needed there though, only great labor, of which an army was a good supply. A thousand hands made light work of the toil.

As it was in the outside of the fortress, so it was on the inside. Enormous amounts of work had been done there to clean floors, remove vermin, repair benches and roofs and windows. It was now weatherproof, and the warriors had a place to rest when not fighting on the walls. Even an ancient brewery had been discovered and cleaned, and now beer was being fermented. The men would have the comforts of home while the enemy suffered the elements.

Every day, winter drew closer. Kubodin looked forward to it. And he dreaded it. The cold would kill the enemy as well as swords. Even so, it might be his own greatest enemy. Such hardship among the Nagraks might force the shamans into using magic. That was what he feared above all. What then of ramparts and gates and the courage of the defenders?

23. Old Men of the Dim Past

Shar considered Asana's question. *Are we trapped in this valley now?* She wished that were the greatest of the problems ahead of her.

"There's a way out. Basically, the same way we came in, but there are pillars at intervals around the valley so our exit need not be by the same set. The shamans will guard it anyway. Getting out isn't a problem. It's being *allowed* to leave that might be. In truth, who knows how the shamans Shulu trapped here will feel about me?"

There was not much else to tell them, and after their deadly trials they were exhausted. They slept after that, and they were too tired to even establish a watch. That worried Shar, for surely the shamans would have sensed something of the magic that she had invoked, and seen the enchantment leap from pillar to pillar around the valley. They would know what it meant. Even so, sleep took her like the rest.

It was dawn when she woke, and the others were already up. They ate a swift breakfast, and cast uneasy glances around them. The fog was still there, as thick as ever.

The sun had risen though, and even if they could not see far it gave a silvery cast to the swirling mists, and they seemed less sinister than last night.

There was only one direction to go, and that was downhill toward the center of the valley where the shamans had likely made their home. What it would look like, and how many of them still lived, Shar did not know, but she led the way with a confident step. Leadership was as much about giving an impression of surety as it was of making the right decisions.

They had not gone far when the fog ceased abruptly. It was almost like walking through a doorway into another room, quite different from the previous one. Here was green grass, and sun, and birds greeting the rising dawn from bushes and trees.

"Look behind us," Huigar said.

Shar turned and looked. The fog really was like a wall, and it towered up behind them as though it were a sheer cliff face.

She glanced skyward. The heavens were blue, but there was a glimmer of fog there, somewhat like a thin veil that covered all. The magic encompassed the entire valley, and there was no escape from the enchantment at any corner, nor by constructing something to climb out of it. Likely, too, the magic penetrated the earth so that no tunnels could be mined for escape. When Shulu did something, she did it properly.

The valley was larger than it seemed from outside, and from their high point they had a good view of it. The grass was a verdant green, even this time of year. There were woods aplenty, and several streams feeding a creek, which in turn, emptied into a lake at the center. There would be game here, and fertile soil. In truth, if it were a prison then it would be a joy to suffer confinement here.

The rebel shamans would not see it like that though. Of them, there was little sign. Shar looked, but she saw no paths, nor cut trees, nor evidence of mining for clay or metals. There was no sign that anyone dwelled here at all.

As they walked though, there became visible a plume of smoke coming from the center of the valley near the lake. It was far away, but there was likely a village there. That would be the place to establish it, by sources of fresh flowing water that were good to drink, and near the still waters of the lake that should harbor abundant fish as a supply of food.

They continued on, ever downhill. The pursuit that had harried them held no fear now, so they took their time. Time was something they had in abundance too. However long they spent here, little or none of it would pass in the outside world. Even so, Shar felt a deep anxiety to return to her army and Kubodin. He would lead it well, but unless she was wrong, then they would be facing great trouble very soon.

The slope of the land lessened somewhat, and they entered a country that was deeper of soil and that grew even thicker grass. There were signs that cattle had grazed here recently, and sheep also at some time before that. Without doubt, some of the shamans were still alive.

Radatan led them again now, for Shar had no better knowledge of what was in the valley than he did.

"Time for lunch," the hunter said, and they stopped and ate a little of their food.

"This is a fine valley," Huigar said. "Have you considered that maybe the shamans would not want to leave here, even when freedom is offered?"

Shar had not thought of that before. "An interesting idea. I hope you're wrong though."

It was a concern. There were so many reasons why the shamans would reject helping her, and this was just one more. Still, they were men of power. However much they liked it here, it was still a prison and she thought they would like to exercise their power in the real world and influence others. That was what men of power had always wanted.

They kept going after that, and as evening drew on they were on flat lands now toward the bottom of the valley. There was still no sign of people, but the column of smoke had gone up unceasing through the day, and increased now as the time for an evening meal approached.

The travelers established a camp, but they lit no fire of their own. The presence of a stranger in the valley must be known, but Shar preferred to come to the shamans on her own terms rather than as a captured prisoner.

They slept, but this time they kept a guard. The first watch went to Shar, and when it was done Asana took over. She slept deeply, and it did not seem that long before a pair of hands woke her, gently shaking her shoulder.

"Someone is coming," Radatan whispered in her ear.

She stood and looked around. Asana and Huigar were just getting up too. It was still dark, but not the full blackness of night. The sky to the east was gray, and in the distance she heard the calls of some birds she did not recognize.

The land seemed peaceful, yet there was a menace there. Soon she heard a noise, and she knew it for a boot that stood upon a branch and cracked it. The silence deepened, and then a voice broke it.

"Hello the camp!"

They gave no answer, but the whisper of their swords from the sheaths was loud in the pre-dawn quiet.

"You won't need those," the voice called again.

A few moments later a figure emerged from the dimness. He seemed alone, but if he had companions perhaps they were quieter than he was. Shar did not think he did, though.

The figure came closer, hands held loosely by his side, without any glint of a weapon. Shar could see him fairly clearly now. He was an old man. Very old, judging by his silver hair and long, white beard. Yet he walked without trouble, and seemed spritely. His robes, for he wore robes rather than trousers and a tunic, were white and about his waist was a simple rope belt.

As he came even closer, she saw that she was wrong. His hands were not empty, and in one of them he held a staff. It was not raised though.

He had the look of a shaman about him. There was something in his eyes that reminded Shar of Shulu. He had power, but it was veiled. In that, he was very much like Shulu.

Yet no shaman that Shar had ever heard tell of had ever used a staff. That was the mark of the wizards of other lands, chiefly to the south and east. He came to a stop and leaned on it, gazing at them. Not only was he unusual for a shaman, he was not like other Cheng. Instantly she was reminded of Asana. Here was a man whose lineage was not only Cheng but also of the men of the east. Despite all this, he spoke the Cheng language, even if with an air of antiquity like a story passed down through the centuries.

He looked straight at her then. "Welcome to Nathradin Valley, Shar Fei."

Shar felt a jolt of surprise run right through her. "How could you possibly know my name?"

He laughed. "We are shamans, and we know many things. Did you think that when the descendent of Chen Fei, he who imprisoned us, came to plead for our help that we would not divine who she was and what she wanted?"

"In all honesty?" Shar replied. "It did *not* occur to me that you would do so."

She would not allow his other comment to go unchallenged. It might provoke a fight, but the truth was the truth and only by accepting it might there be a chance of working together.

"And while it's true that the emperor had you imprisoned here, it was only after you betrayed him. What did you expect after such a thing?"

She saw Huigar pale a little at those words. It was a confrontational way of trying to start negotiations, but if she surrendered ground now she would be on the back foot from the very start.

Huigar did not just pale. She moved a step or two closer to Shar, and Radatan did likewise. They took their role as guards seriously. Only Asana remained where he was. He seemed relaxed and tranquil, as he always did. Even so, his hand was close to the hilt of his sword, and Shar knew that if trouble began he would be the fastest of them all to react.

The shaman missed none of what was happening, and his gaze moved across them all taking in everything. He made no hostile move though, and merely smiled as if expecting exactly this.

"Come, this is not the time nor place for such a discussion. I'm early, and you have not broken your fast yet. Eat, and then we'll be on our way. They're expecting you at the village."

There was no point in doing anything other than what the shaman said, so they had their breakfast and invited him to join them. He did so, but there was little conversation.

A short while later it was broad daylight, and the shaman led them away from their camp toward the village. There was a path to follow, little more than a track, but it widened after a mile. Evidently, the shamans did not travel far from the village too often. There was probably little need, for the water and fertile soil was at the bottom, and they had livestock to take advantage of it. Probably the higher ground at the valley sides was only occasionally used for grazing, and probably even less frequently for hunting.

"You say they are expecting us?" Shar asked the shaman.

"Indeed. And much will be discussed."

"And then?"

The shaman did not break his stride. "Then you will all be put to the death. Or we will help you. It will be one or the other."

Shar did not miss a step either. She had been blunt with him, and he now returned the favor. Also, it occurred to her that this was a kind of testing. If, by chance, the renegade shamans agreed to help her they would first assess whether or not she had a chance of beating their brethren outside the valley. A leader dismayed by the threat of death would be seen as weak, so she merely smiled and walked on with him, stride for stride.

"Do you really know why I've come, and what help I'll request?" she asked.

"There are those among us who have some measure of foresight. Not enough for us to avoid being caught in this trap of Shulu Gan," and for the first time his voice held a tone of bitterness, "and besides that, Shulu Gan herself told us that one day a descendent of Chen Fei might come."

That was yet another surprise to Shar. She knew that Shulu was not especially gifted at foretelling, and yet she was not without skill either. How much of current events had her magic shown her all those years ago? How much had she seen since then?

She tried for a bit of surprise herself. "And do you know how Chen Fei died?"

The shaman glanced at her as they walked, and she could see an element of curiosity. They did not know.

"He was assassinated. Betrayed by Olekhai, his prime minister. Killed by poison, and yet even in death the shamans fled from him in fear."

There was a strange look on the man's face. In part, she read it as satisfaction. That did not bode well for her. Yet there was also a passing shadow of regret.

Perhaps there was hope for her yet with these shamans, but she would have to prove to them that she was all the things Chen Fei was, less what they did not like about him. It was a narrow path to tread.

24. Are You Worthy?

"Tell me," the shaman asked. "You are descended from Chen Fei, and we know in this valley that Shulu Gan's magic invokes time. How long has passed outside since we were imprisoned here?"

It was a dangerous question. The truth might provoke the shamans beyond all reason, yet the truth was the truth and it would come out sooner or later.

"Give or take," Shar replied. "It's been a thousand years."

The shaman glanced at her quickly, raising his bushy eyebrows.

"Really? That's fascinating. To us, it has been but a few score years. We have had different theories on the time variance, and this news will set all arguments to rest. One of us in particular will be pleased. He calculated a figure close to that, but the rest disputed his reasoning."

It was not the reaction Shar expected at all. It was one of pure academic interest, and she realized that these shamans were not like others she had met. She could not predict their reactions, and did not know what might be trivial or important to them. It made her task even harder.

They soon entered an area of land that showed signs of habitation. Cattle lowed and sheep bleated in the distance. The smell of smoke was in the air, and here and there were indications the earth had been tilled at times, even if it was fallow now.

The village was not yet visible. They followed a well beaten path by the creek, and came to a marshy area where it fed into the lake. This they skirted on its southern shore, and Shar soon saw boats tethered to a kind of jetty. No one was on them though, nor was there any person visible anywhere.

"Where are the people?" Shar asked.

"Gathered and waiting," the shaman replied. "You will see them soon, and then all will be decided."

True to his word they soon passed through a thick wood that partially flanked this side of the lake, and on the other side they could now see the village.

Just as the shaman was not like other shamans, or even Cheng people, so it was with the village. It consisted of a cluster of buildings, rectangular in shape and steep roofed, built of dressed timber rather than the cruder round huts favored by the Cheng.

Most strange of all though was the main building. It too was steep roofed and rectangular, but it was quite long. Shar had heard stories of this type of house. On the other side of the Eagle Claw Mountains were a people known as Duthenor, and their chiefs lived in buildings such as this, which they called long halls.

There were gardens now, irrigated by channels linking to the lake, and a pathway of stones, neatly laid, that ran to the front of the hall.

The shaman led them to the great front door of the building, made of hewn timber and looking strong enough to withstand an attack of great force. Two guards stood there, and they were shamans but they seemed a little younger than the one who led the travelers. Each held a staff as did he though, and it looked to Shar as though they wished to use them. She did not like the looks these men gave her. There was more than a hint of anger in them.

Their guide led them into the hall, and the two guards closed the door behind them, coming in also.

It was a strange building to Shar. The floor was of timber, yet a long pit had been left in the middle in which a great log burned. On the sides were trestle tables, where the shamans must eat. But now they were gathered near the head of the hall. There a kind of dais had been built, and three chairs were set there, occupied by three shamans, who must be the elders. These men looked at Shar sternly, and the glances of many that stood before the dais were hostile as well.

Shar walked proudly, and she ignored the resentment. Yet when she came before the dais she offered an inclination of her head to the three elders. She would not bow and be subservient, yet she would also show them due respect.

The man sitting in the center chair spoke. "Welcome to our prison, Shar Fei, daughter of the line of Chen Fei. Welcome, and tell us why we should not kill you."

Just as their guide had been, this elder came straight to the point. It was intended to intimidate. It was part of her testing, and she knew it for such. Had they determined to kill her already, they would have just attacked.

If they wanted to be blunt, she could do that as well as they.

"Because I can set you free. Kill me, and you will never leave this valley, and it will end up being your grave just as it is mine."

The elder studied her, and she studied him in turn. He was old. Ancient even, and his white beard was straggly as the hair on his head. The hand that held the staff was withered, yet it still kept a firm grip of the wood.

"Mayhap we could use torture to wrest the secret from you, and escape of our own accord."

Shar laughed, and she felt the glance of her three companions on her. What happened to her would likely happen to them, and they were surprised by her reaction.

"Mayhap," she replied. "I'll save you the trouble though. I'll tell you the secret of the magic freely, for all the good it will do you."

She took a step closer to the elder, and looked him straight in the eye.

"The Swords of Dawn and Dusk are they keys. It's their magic that interacts with the enchantment over this valley, and opens a gateway. Their magic, and theirs alone. And only I can invoke it. My hands on the swords and my voice. You could wring from me the spell, but what good is that if you cannot touch the swords?"

The old man said nothing. He seemed neither pleased nor disappointed, but merely thoughtful. At his left, another elder leaned forward.

"Shulu Gan prepared the trap well, but there are ways that even dead hands can be made to hold the swords."

Shar nodded. "Perhaps. But the magic in the swords and gates … is sentient. It cannot be tricked. The gate will only open if I command it, and in the right way."

Shar was on tricky ground here. Shulu had told her much, but she had surmised some of this too. She might be wrong, but she did not want to put it to the test. Likewise, the shamans must have experimented on the enchantment to try to break free. They would know by now that it was sentient, but it was better if they did not know how that was achieved. The sooner this conversation moved to the next step, the happier she would be. Even so, she stood calmly before the three elders, her arms folded.

The third elder spoke. "Have you considered that maybe we are happy here, and will not choose to leave, even if we could?"

"It's a pleasant valley," Shar replied. "More than that. It's beautiful. Even so, I don't think you'll choose to do that. If I'm wrong though, I've come here on a fool's errand, and may die for it. Worse, the Cheng nation will suffer because of my mistake."

The first elder spoke again. "What transpires in the outside world?"

This was a start. These men had broken away from their brethren at the time of Chen Fei because they did not think the goals of the shamans were right. Now that those goals were implemented, it would give them a chance to see that they were right, and that might sway them to her side.

"It's been a thousand years since the shamans murdered Chen Fei. They have ruled since then with an iron fist. Tribe is set against tribe. That way they fight each other and don't unite to overthrow the shamans. Poverty is rife. Superstition abounds. The sciences of building, medicine, farming and many others have regressed. The people are lied to about everything, and they know it, but fear to speak lest the nazram are sent to their homes. Traitors are called heroes, and villains are put forward for veneration. The truth is made to stand on its head, and lies are spoken unashamedly as the truth. Does this sound familiar to you? It should. It all happened in your time too, before Chen Fei rose to power."

"And there is a rebellion against it?" the first elder asked.

"Since I revealed myself, many tribes have joined me. There have been battles. I won them. There will be more, and those I may win also. I have only one great fear. It might be my undoing, but nothing is certain."

"And that is?"

"My enemies possess magic. And they use it against warriors. It's against decency and all tradition, but still they do it."

This caused a stir among the rebel shamans, but only the elder spoke.

"And does not Shulu protect you against them? Does she not still live?"

"She lives, but I don't know where she is. In short, I need shamans to help protect my army from shamans. I need *you*. Serve me in this conflict, and I'll set you free."

The elder on the left spoke, and his words were harsh and his expression cold.

"All this, or most of it, we already know. Some of it from of old, and some by our soothsayers. But none of it matters."

"Why not?" Shar asked, and she felt her stomach sinking.

"Because you must prove yourself worthy of the land. For none other than the savior of the Cheng nation will we abase ourselves to serve. So you must be tested, and if you fail you will die."

Shar did not like the sound of this, but she had expected as much and stood proudly before them. She would do what was required, and succeed in getting these people's help. No matter the cost.

"So be it. What is your test? I will pass it."

The first elder spoke, and his voice was mild. Perhaps it even held sympathy.

"You must fight someone. If you don't beat him, he will kill you."

Shar shrugged. "It would not be the first time. Who is it?"

The first elder gently shook his head. "It *will* be a first. You have never fought someone like this before. He has never lost a battle. We anticipate his strength and skill to be greater than yours. He cannot lose."

"I will beat him, nevertheless," Shar replied.

Many of the shamans in the hall laughed, but the first elder merely gazed at her, and this time there was definitely sympathy in his eyes.

"Who is it?" she asked.

25. To the Death

The first elder answered Shar's question. "Who it is, you will soon discover. For now, let us leave this hall. It is not a suitable place for the testing."

He led the way, and Shar and her companions followed. The rest of the shamans came after, until the entire hall was emptied and some fifty of the strange old men were gathered outside.

There was a clearing before the hall, where no tree nor bush stood. The ground was flat and covered by a sward of short green grass. Through the middle ran the pathway of stones, but the first elder led them to the left of this. Here, it felt different. Shar could not tell in what manner, except that she sensed magic. More than magic perhaps. It was a sacred place, hallowed by prayer, or perhaps visited by a god. It reminded her of Uhrum, and what it felt like when she had spoken to Kubodin during his rite of passage to chieftainship.

"Do you agree to our terms?" the first elder asked.

"What are they?" Shar replied.

"Does it matter? You must accept them, and pass the test, otherwise we will not aid you."

Shar did not like it, but she had little choice. "Very well."

"Then these are the terms. You cannot use the Swords of Dawn and Dusk. This will be a fight to the death. No mercy will be shown, and no quarter given. Do you agree?"

"I agree," Shar said firmly. "Who is my opponent?"

"Your opponent has many names. Among the Cheng, he is most widely known as Cragamasta."

Shar felt a cold stab of fear. "You would have me fight one of the gods? The god of battle and war himself?"

"That is the test, decided long ago when first we were imprisoned, and when our soothsayers foretold your coming. You must fight a god, and win. However, it is not too late to decline. You may do so, and the lives of your friends shall be spared. Though you, we may still put to death."

"And if I fight, but lose, will you spare my friends?"

The elders discussed that in whispers among themselves.

"We agree to that."

Asana spoke out, and there was a restrained anger in his voice. It was one of the few times she had seen him allow his emotions to show.

"This is madness. Shar is a great fighter, but no one can contend against a god!"

Shar had the feeling that if anyone could, it might be Asana, but he misconstrued the test. It was not one of fighting skill, but of courage and will. They wanted to know that she was prepared to sacrifice her life for the Cheng people. That was why they had left her the hope of life, if she was not. It made the test all the harder to proceed with.

"Hush, my friend," she said. "This is their test, and I'll win because I must. Have no fear. Not for me, at least. Reserve it for the Cheng nation if I'm killed."

The shamans then formed a great ring about the sward of grass, and the first elder signaled Shar to lay down the Swords of Dawn and Dusk. This she did, placing them well out of the way. Then one of the shamans approached, and handed her a single sword. It was of good construction, and similar in size and shape to what she was used to. She would dearly miss the swords that Shulu had fashioned though.

Soon, the shamans began to chant, and Shar looked at her friends. They stood together in one place, and their gazes were on her. They did not speak, but she saw the love in their eyes, and their fear. She placed her hand on her heart to signify what she felt for them, and then looked away. She must prepare for what was to come without distraction.

The grass seemed very green to her, and the sky so very blue. She felt the sunlight on her face, and the stirring of a breeze that caressed her skin. A dove called from the roof of the long hall, and she felt perspiration bead on her face.

Deep was the chanting of the shamans, and in its way it was beautiful. It reminded Shar of Shulu, for sometimes she chanted to invoke magic, but this was a chorus of strong voices, and it lifted heavenwards in a rumble as though thunder spoke with a voice.

The sky answered. A grumble echoed back and rolled through the valley. The dove stopped calling, and the breeze died.

At that moment, the shamans suddenly ceased and went down as one upon bended knee. Shar stood, relaxed and waiting.

There was a flash in the sky, and a light that dazzled the eyes. She held up a hand to shield them, and when the light faded, she saw a new figure opposite her on the sward. Shulu had told her what this god looked like, but her description had not readied her for the sense of awe that she felt.

With difficulty, she stopped herself from genuflecting as the shamans did. This was her opponent, and she could not start the contest by acknowledging his authority.

Instead, she must focus on one thing, and one thing alone. Defeating him.

Cragamasta was tall, standing at some seven feet. He wore armor of a strange design, with shoulder plates, greaves and vambraces that were spiked and twisted backward, and the metal gleamed as though it were made of polished silver. His helm covered his head, but not his face, and it swept back also but in the design of eagle wings. His armor looked heavy, and yet when he glanced around him at the shamans, his movements seemed easy and lithe.

The piercing glance of the god fell upon her, and now she felt the full force of that awe which he wore as a mantle. It weighed upon her like a mountain, and began to force her to her knees.

Instead, she spoke.

"Hail, Cragamasta. I respect you as a god, yet still I will fight you. And win."

The god studied her, and a faint grin came to his handsome face.

"Hail, Shar Fei, emperor that *might* be. The appointed hour has come when we must fight, as long ago it was foreseen. You will prove yourself worthy to continue your quest, or you will die."

His voice was soft and subtle, yet still full of strength. Shar liked it. He did not sound, nor look, quite as she had thought he would. Shulu had told her little of him, and she wondered if that had been deliberate. Had she known this day would come? Was that why she had been reticent to speak of him? Or maybe it was chance, for Shulu had not described all the gods in detail.

"If I die," she replied to him, "no one will say that I did not still fight with all I have. Even against a god with divine powers."

Cragamasta cocked his head, and then looked at the shamans.

"You did not tell her?"

"No," answered the first elder, not looking the god in the eyes. "That was the first part of the test, to see if fear could induce her to give up the quest."

"Cruel, but effective," Cragamasta replied.

He bent his gaze on Shar again. "Know, mortal, that I bear you no malice. Among thens, there are those who wish you to succeed, and those who do not. It does not matter what I think. I am merely the instrument of this test, requested by the shamans and agreed to by all the gods. We must fight, and only one can prevail. Yet know this also. I have taken mortal form. I can be beaten, and I cannot use any of my powers, save my prowess at arms. Yet you will discover that even in this form my skill surpasses any you have fought before."

Shar felt a wave of hope rush through her. Determination alone had driven her before, but now she knew that victory was indeed possible, even if a remote chance. That was a chance she would take, and nothing would hold her back from winning.

"Then it will be a fair fight," she said. "And when I have won, you may return to the gods and tell them that the blood of Chen Fei runs true and bold in my veins."

"That, we will see," Cragamasta said, and he drew his sword from its sheath. The blade was silver as was his armor, and the hilts came back as eagle wings like his helm. The look in his eye was that of an eagle too, sharp and intent.

The god attacked first, and he leaped at her with a thrust. She danced away, barely in time, and he pursued relentlessly.

Sword clashed against sword now, and strive as she might she was not quick enough to deflect instead of parry. It would be a short battle unless she could change that, for he was stronger than she was.

Shar feinted, pretending to attack his legs so that she might swivel the tip of the blade around and strike for the neck. She knew already that he was a superb fighter, and he would read that trick as though it were a book and reply with a straight thrust at her body and so kill her before her blade took the longer circular route. On this she gambled.

Even as the straight thrust came for her, she twisted to the side, abandoning her strike with the blade and instead kicking out with her leg at the god's knee.

Her boot made contact, and she drove it with force and put her weight behind it. It was a bone breaking technique, and one that she had practiced under Shulu's tutelage since her childhood.

It nearly worked, but even as her weight descended the god collapsed his knee and absorbed much of the blow. Shar jumped back, and did so only just in time to avoid a slash that would have beheaded her.

Cragamasta gazed at her, and she sensed his surprise. He was more skilled than she, and yet she was still a threat to him. With luck, she could win.

He charged at her, sword flashing. It was not a rush of anger, but cool and calculated. This time, she managed to hold her own and use soft hands to deflect. Then she realized that despite his speed, he was not quite as fast as before. At first, she thought he must be growing tired, but then she saw it. He limped slightly on the leg that she had attacked, and though her kick had not broken bones or dislocated the joint as intended, it had still caused an injury.

She tried to take advantage of that. Deflecting an overhand strike, she sidestepped to come in from his side, hoping that the injury would prevent him from turning as swiftly as she.

The god surprised her though, spinning rapidly, even if it was done with a groan, and his sword leaped out. She was too slow to get her blade into position, but she leaned back and felt the whisper of death near her neck.

Shar pivoted and retreated.

The god pursued her, and he was calm yet determined. Blow after blow rained upon her. Strike after strike. Thrust after thrust, and each movement brought her close to death, yet she deflected them all, or else retreated.

And she turned retreat into a kind of offence, knowing that each step she forced her opponent to take was a movement that troubled his injury further and brought him pain. For one thing she was sure of, god as he was, he had spoken the truth and in this mortal form would feel any hurt. She had heard that in his groan, and seen it in his limp.

Retreating was not enough. She never went back in a straight line but rather took turns at veering from side to side, all the more to put pressure on his knee.

Even so, his skill showed, and a blow arced before her neck and in avoiding that she did not see until too late the kick that drove into her stomach. She reeled back, struggling for air, and the god fell upon her in a whirlwind of sword strokes that flashed as lightning.

Shar fell. Behind the bright light of the sword of Cragamasta it seemed that the world gathered up in a massive bank of black clouds, and her doom was upon her and her failure of the Cheng nation was as a wave of regret about to collapse upon her.

The god struck. It was the last blow. She lay on her back, and the eagle-hilted sword descended. Nothing would stop it, for Cragamasta drove the tip down with all his weight behind it. As though from some great distance, she heard the moan of Asana, and the cries of Radatan and Huigar.

Like lightning, the blow fell. But that coolness of mind that overcame Shar at times of peril descended over her. Time slowed. Her perception of reality changed. This was the perfect state of Stillness in the Storm that warriors sought, and she recognized that she had fully achieved it, yet no emotion came with that understanding. It was what it was, and the world was nothing more than a mote of dust floating in vastness, and the sword about to take her life was nothing compared to that mote. All things were possible. One moment of time such as this could stretch for eternity, and the cosmos was so large that the mind could not encompass it, or so small that it could all fit at the point of the sword.

That point came downward. Shar was one with it. She knew it as she knew her every breath and move. It plummeted, touching her stomach, but already she was rolling. The blade bit deep, and found nothing but the ground to plunge into.

Time returned as a flood of events. She heard the gasps of the crowd watching, and felt the sting of the blade where it drew blood from her skin in passing into the earth. She felt the weight of her sword, and the momentum of it as it arced through the air. Then she felt its impact.

The point of her sword took Cragamasta in the neck, above his armor and below his helm. Blood sprayed, and he staggered back.

Shar rolled and came to her feet in a crouched stance, ready for anything. But the battle was done.

Cragamasta fell to his knees, and astonishment was on his face. Then the blood flowing from his neck turned from red to gold, from liquid to light. The light grew in brightness until it was blinding, then flickered away.

The body of the god lay on the grass before her, dead. It sunk into the ground and was gone, but above it stood the true Cragamasta, a spirit wreathed in a golden light, sword in hand and awe about him as though he were the first dawn to ever rise over the earth. She remembered then that he was the son of Uhrum, and she saw the resemblance.

Cragamasta sheathed his sword. "By the gods," he declaimed, glancing at the shamans, "I declare Shar Fei the victor. Destiny is one with her, and she with it. If she becomes emperor of the Cheng peoples, they will have no coward as a leader, but a woman of fire, steel and courage." He turned his glance upon Shar. "And I am pleased. I fought with all the skill of that mortal body, for such was the duty appointed me. Yet I am one among the gods who hoped you would win. So it has come to pass, but remember others among the gods wish your death."

Cragamasta raised up his arms, and the golden light flared like a thousand suns. When Shar could see again, he was gone. Turning to the shamans, she surveyed them.

They would not kill her now. She would lead them from the valley and free them. But what then? Would they agree to help her only to betray her as they had done her forefather?

Thus ends *Swords of Shadow*. The Shaman's Sword series continues in book five, *Swords of Wrath*, where Shar's conflict with the shamans heightens, and the battle of freedom against tyranny begins in earnest…

SWORDS OF WRATH

BOOK FIVE OF THE SHAMAN'S SWORD SERIES

COMING SOON!

Amazon lists millions of titles, and I'm glad you discovered this one. But if you'd like to know when I release a new book, instead of leaving it to chance, sign up for my new release list. I'll send you an email on publication.

Yes please! – Go to www.homeofhighfantasy.com and sign up.

No thanks – I'll take my chances.

Dedication

There's a growing movement in fantasy literature. Its name is noblebright, and it's the opposite of grimdark.

Noblebright celebrates the virtues of heroism. It's an old-fashioned thing, as old as the first story ever told around a smoky campfire beneath ancient stars. It's storytelling that highlights courage and loyalty and hope for the spirit of humanity. It recognizes the dark, the dark in us all, and the dark in the villains of its stories. It recognizes death, and treachery and betrayal. But it dwells on none of these things.

I dedicate this book, such as it is, to that which is noblebright. And I thank the authors before me who held the torch high so that I could see the path: J.R.R. Tolkien, C.S. Lewis, Terry Brooks, Susan Cooper, Roger Taylor and many others. I salute you.

And, for a time, I too shall hold the torch high.

Appendix: Encyclopedic Glossary

Note: The history of the Cheng Empire is obscure, for the shamans hid much of it. Yet the truth was recorded in many places and passed down in family histories, in secret societies and especially among warrior culture. This glossary draws on much of that 'secret' history, and each book in this series is individualized to reflect the personal accounts that have come down through the dark tracts of time to the main actors within each book's pages. Additionally, there is often historical material provided in its entries for people, artifacts and events that are not included in the main text.

Many races dwell in Alithoras. All have their own language, and though sometimes related to one another the changes sparked by migration, isolation and various influences often render these tongues unintelligible to each other.

The ascendancy of Halathrin culture across the land, who are sometimes called elves, combined with their widespread efforts to secure and maintain allies against various evil incursions, has made their language the primary means of communication between diverse peoples. This was especially so during the Shadowed Wars, but has persisted through the centuries afterward.

This glossary contains a range of names and terms. Some are of Halathrin origin, and their meaning is provided.

The Cheng culture is also revered by its people, and many names are given in their tongue. It is important to remember that the empire was vast though, and there is no one Cheng language but rather a multitude of dialects. Perfect consistency of spelling and meaning is therefore not to be looked for.

List of abbreviations:

Cam. Camar

Chg. Cheng

Comb. Combined

Cor. Corrupted form

Hal. Halathrin

Prn. Pronounced

Anakabael: A slave of the shaman Drogul, captured from lands to the south.

Aranloth's age: An exclamation in use in various areas of Alithoras. Aranloth is a lòhren, and said to have been born before the Shadowed Wars. The exclamation suggests great surprise or astonishment.

Argash: *Chg.* "The clamor of war." Once a warrior of the Fen Wolf Tribe, and leader of a band of the leng-fah. Now chief of the clan.

Asana: *Chg.* "Gift of light." Rumored to be the greatest swordmaster in the history of the Cheng people. His father was a Duthenor tribesman from outside the bounds of the old Cheng Empire.

Chen Fei: *Chg.* "Graceful swan." Swans are considered birds of wisdom and elegance in Cheng culture. It is said that one flew overhead at the time of Chen's birth, and his mother named him for it. He rose from poverty to become emperor of his people, and he was loved by many but despised by some. He was warrior, general, husband, father, poet, philosopher, painter, but most of all he was enemy to the machinations of the shamans who tried to secretly govern all aspects of the people.

Cheng: *Chg.* "Warrior." The overall name of the various related tribes united by Chen Fei. It was a word for warrior in his dialect, later adopted for his growing army and last of all for the people of his nation. His empire disintegrated after his assassination, but much of the culture he fostered endured.

Cheng Empire: A vast array of realms formerly governed by kings and united, briefly, under Chen Fei. One of the largest empires ever to rise in Alithoras.

Conclave of Shamans: The government of the shamans, consisting of several elders and their chosen assistants.

Cragamasta: *Chg.* "The bull that charges." A god of the Cheng pantheon, associated with war, battle and thunderstorms.

Dakashul: *Chg.* "Stallion of two colors – a piebald." Chief of the Iron Dog Clan.

Damril: *Chg.* "Slender sapling." A warrior of the Green Hornet Tribe.

Drogul: *Chg.* "The wolf that howls at the moon." Seventh Elder of the Conclave of Shamans.

Duthenor: A tribe on the other side of the Eagle Claw Mountains, unrelated to the Cheng. They are breeders of cattle and herders of sheep. Said to be great warriors, and rumor holds that Asana is partly of their blood.

Eagle Claw Mountains: A mountain range toward the south of the Cheng Empire. It is said the people who later became the Cheng lived here first and over centuries moved out to populate the surrounding lands. Others believe that these people were blue-eyed, and intermixed with various other races as they came down off the mountains to trade and make war.

Elù-haraken: *Hal.* "The shadowed wars." Long ago battles in a time that is become myth to the Cheng tribes.

Fen Wolf Tribe: A tribe that live in Tsarin Fen. Once, they and the neighboring Soaring Eagle Tribe were one people and part of a kingdom. It is also told that Chen Fei was born in that realm.

Fields of Rah: Rah signifies "ocean of the sky" in many Cheng dialects. It is a country of vast grasslands but at its center is Nagrak City, which of old was the capital of the empire. It was in this city that the emperor was assassinated.

Forest of Dreams: A forest in the northwest of the Cheng lands. Sometimes said to be haunted, but certainly known to be the dwelling place of many creatures of magic driven out of more populated lands. A place of danger that even shamans avoid.

Gan: *Chg.* "They who have attained." It is an honorary title added to a person's name after they have acquired great skill. It can be applied to warriors, shamans, sculptors, weavers or any particular expertise. It is reserved for the greatest of the best.

Ghirlock: *Chg.* "The goat that flies." A bird of the snipe species. Associated with the supernatural and the elemental gods of the Cheng. Its sound in flight is like the bleat of a goat.

Go Shan: *Chg.* "Daughter of wisdom." An epithet of Shulu Gan.

Gnarhash: *Chg.* "The clamor of hail." A warrior of the Iron Dog Clan.

Green Hornet Clan: A grassland clan immediately to the west of the Wahlum Hills. Their numbers are relatively small, but they are famous for their use of venomed arrows and especially darts.

Halathrin: *Hal.* "People of Halath." A race of elves named after an honored lord who led an exodus of his people to the land of Alithoras in pursuit of justice, having sworn to defeat a great evil. They are human, though of fairer form, greater skill and higher culture. They possess a unity of body, mind and spirit that enables insight and endurance beyond the native races of Alithoras. Said to be immortal, but killed in great numbers during their conflicts in ancient times with the evil they sought to destroy. Those conflicts are collectively known as the Shadowed Wars.

Heart of the Hurricane: The shamans' term for the state of mind warriors call Stillness in the Storm. See that term for further information.

Huigar: *Chg.* "Mist on the mountain peak." A bodyguard to Shar. Daughter of the chief of the Smoking Eyes Clan, and a swordsperson of rare skill.

Iron Dog Clan: A tribe of the Wahlum Hills. So named for their legendary endurance and determination.

Kubodin: *Chg.* Etymology unknown. A wild warrior from the Wahlum Hills, and chief of the Two Ravens Clan. Simple appearing, but far more than he seems. Asana's manservant and friend.

Lòhren: *Hal. Prn.* Ler-ren. "Knowledge giver – a counselor." Other terms used by various nations include sage, wizard, and druid.

Magic: Mystic power.

Magrig: Name of unknown origin. A young, but highly competent, warrior of the Smoking Eyes Tribe. Despite his youth, said to have fought several duels after his heritage was questioned.

Nahring: *Chg.* "White on the lake – mist." Chief of the Smoking Eyes Clan, and father of Huigar. Rumor persists that his family possesses some kind of magic, but if so it has never been publicly revealed.

Nagga-snagga birds: *Chg.* "Smelly-greedy." A species of ibis.

Nagrak: *Chg.* "Those who follow the herds." A Cheng tribe that dwell on the Fields of Rah. Traditionally they lived a nomadic lifestyle, traveling in the wake of herds of wild cattle that provided all their needs. But an element of their tribe, and some contend this was another tribe in origin that they conquered, are great builders and live in a city.

Nagrak City: A great city at the heart of the Fields of Rah. Once the capital of the Cheng Empire.

Nagralak Village: A small village on the Fields of Rah. Named after a famous warrior during the Shadowed Wars.

Nakatath: *Chg.* "Emperor-to-be." A term coined by Chen Fei and used by him during the period where he sought to bring the Cheng tribes together into one nation. It is said that it deliberately mocked the shamans, for they used the term *Nakolbrin* to signify an apprentice shaman ready to ascend to full authority.

Nathradin (the vale of): Variously translated as vale of howling winds or vale of screaming spirits. A valley within the mostly flat Fields of Rah. It is claimed a great battle was fought here, before even the time of the Shadowed Wars.

Nazram: *Chg.* "The wheat grains that are prized after the chaff is excluded." An elite warrior organization that is in service to the shamans. For the most part, they are selected from those who quest for the twin swords each triseptium, though there are exceptions to this.

Nightbringer Canyons: Deep canyons in the far west of the Cheng lands.

Night Walker Clan: A tribe of the Wahlum Hills. The name derives from their totem animal, which is a nocturnal predator of thick forests. It's a type of cat, small but fierce and covered in black fur.

Olekhai: *Chg.* "The falcon that plummets." A famous and often used name in the old world before, and during, the Cheng Empire. Never used since the assassination of the emperor, however. The most prominent bearer of the name during the days of the emperor was the chief of his council of wise men. He was, essentially, prime minister of the emperor's government. But he betrayed his lord and his people. Shulu Gan spared his life, but only so as to punish him with a terrible curse.

Quest of Swords: Occurs every triseptium to mark the three times seven years the shamans lived in exile during the emperor's life. The best warriors of each clan seek the twin swords of the emperor. Used by the shamans as a means of finding the most skilled warriors in the land and recruiting them to their service.

Radatan: *Chg.* "The ears that flick – a slang term for deer." A hunter of the Two Ravens Clan.

Sagadar: *Chg.* "Willow tree." Chief of the Night Walker Clan.

Shadowed Wars: See Elù-haraken.

Shaman: The religious leaders of the Cheng people. They are sorcerers, and though the empire is fragmented they work as one across the lands to serve their own united purpose. Their spiritual home is Three Moon Mountain, but few save shamans have ever been there.

Shar: *Chg.* "White stone – the peak of a mountain." A young woman of the Fen Wolf Tribe. Claimed by Shulu Gan to be the descendent of Chen Fei.

Shulu Gan: *Chg.* The first element signifies "magpie." A name given to the then leader of the shamans for her hair was black, save for a streak of white that ran through it.

Smoking Eyes Clan: A tribe of the Wahlum Hills. Named for a god, who they take as their totem.

Soaring Eagle Tribe: A tribe that borders the Fen Wolf clan. At one time, one with them, but now, as is the situation with most tribes, hostilities are common. The eagle is their totem, for the birds are plentiful in the mountain lands to the south and often soar far from their preferred habitat over the tribe's grasslands.

Stillness in the Storm: The state of mind a true warrior seeks in battle. Neither angry nor scared, neither hopeful nor worried. When emotion is banished from the mind, the body is free to express the skill acquired through long years of training. Sometimes also called Calmness in the Storm or the Heart of the Hurricane.

Sun Lo River: *Chg.* "White thunder." A river originating in the Eagle Claw Mountains that, along with the mountains, helps define the southern border of Cheng lands.

Swimming Osprey Clan: A tribe of the Wahlum Hills. Their totem is the osprey, often seen diving into the ocean to catch fish.

Taga Nashu: *Chg.* "The Grandmother who does not die." One of the many epithets of Shulu Gan, greatest of the shamans but cast from their order.

Tagayah: Origin of name unknown. A creature of magic and chaos, born in the old world long before even the Shadowed Wars, but used during those conflicts by the forces of evil.

Tarok: *Chg.* "Head of a deer above tall grass." A warrior of the Soaring Eagle Tribe. Once a nazram, but he left that order of warriors.

Three Moon Mountain: A mountain in the Eagle Claw range. Famed as the home of the shamans. None know what the three moons reference relates to except, perhaps, the shamans.

Triseptium: A period of three times seven years. It signifies the exiles of the shamans during the life of the emperor. Declared by the shamans as a cultural treasure, and celebrated by them. Less so by the tribes, but the shamans encourage it. Much more popular now than in past ages.

Tsarin Fen: *Chg.* Tsarin, which signifies mountain cat, was a general under Chen Fei. It is said he retired to the swamp after the death of his leader. At one time, many regions and villages were named after generals, but the shamans changed the names and did all they could to make people forget the old ones. In their view, all who served the emperor were criminals and their achievements were not to be celebrated. Tsarin Fen is one of the few such names that still survive.

Two Ravens Clan: A tribe of the Wahlum Hills. Their totem is the raven.

Uhrum: *Chg.* "The voice that sings the dawn." Queen of the gods.

Wahlum Hills: *Chg. Comb. Hal.* "Mist-shrouded highlands." Hills to the north-west of the old Cheng empire, and home to Kubodin.

About the author

I'm a man born in the wrong era. My heart yearns for faraway places and even further afield times. Tolkien had me at the beginning of *The Hobbit* when he said, ". . . one morning long ago in the quiet of the world . . ."

Sometimes I imagine myself in a Viking mead-hall. The long winter night presses in, but the shimmering embers of a log in the hearth hold back both cold and dark. The chieftain calls for a story, and I take a sip from my drinking horn and stand up . . .

Or maybe the desert stars shine bright and clear, obscured occasionally by wisps of smoke from burning camel dung. A dry gust of wind marches sand grains across our lonely campsite, and the wayfarers about me stir restlessly. I sip cool water and begin to speak.

I'm a storyteller. A man to paint a picture by the slow music of words. I like to bring faraway places and times to life, to make hearts yearn for something they can never have, unless for a passing moment.